The herd was thundering closer, their pounding hooves causing the ground to quake, when Ki felt the horse stiffen. Then the animal reared up and hung in the air like a statue. Ki grabbed hold of its mane and slid his feet from the stirrups, managing to stay astride.

He knew that the horse might go over on its side, that he might be pinned under it, that it might be better to let himself get thrown from it now. But there was little time to think.

The cattle were almost upon them when the animal lost its balance.

Ki relaxed his body and let go . . .

WESLEY ELLIS

LONE STAR

AND THE TONG'S REVENGE

JOVE BOOKS, NEW YORK

LONE STAR AND THE TONG'S REVENGE

A Jove Book / published by arrangement with
the author

PRINTING HISTORY
Jove edition / July 1987

ISBN: 0-515-09057-3

Jove Books are published by The Berkley Publishing Group,
200 Madison Avenue, New York, New York 10016.
The name "Jove" and the "J" logo
are trademarks belonging to Jove Publications, Inc.

PRINTED IN THE UNITED STATES OF AMERICA

10 9 8 7 6 5 4 3 2 1

For Mike Sobie, without whom none of this
would have been possible

★

Chapter 1

The pressure in the boiler built rapidly. After only a few minutes the locomotive let out a shrill whistle, then chugged out of the water station, leaving behind a trail of black soot and two stranded passengers.

One was a tall, lean man with straight, black hair and a thin mustache. He wore no guns, and his dress, a blue-gray tweed suit with matching shoe-string tie, gave no clue as to his profession. Still, his stance and demeanor said he was not a man to be trifled with.

Under the brim of his Stetson, his almond-shaped eyes surveyed the landscape. His eyes were the strongest indication of his Oriental breeding. From afar, his build, a product of his father, passed him off as American. Sometimes his sallow complexion and long black hair pegged him as an Indian half-breed, but upon looking directly into his face, there was no mistaking the gentle Japanese eyes of his mother. His eyes, however, could be deceiving. Soft as they were, they held no mercy for his enemies or the enemies of his companion.

Ki turned to the woman who stood next to him. There was no way of knowing that this woman, dressed in a silk blouse and brown skirt, could ride and rope with the best of men. She looked to be one of the cultured ladies of San Franscisco. But looks can be so misleading. It wasn't that Jessie lacked culture. On the contrary, she had too many important things to tend to. As head of the Starbuck empire, Jessica Starbuck had little time for "culture." Work always took top priority.

While it was Jessie's job to run the empire, it was Ki's job to look after Jessie. Her well-being was always foremost in his thoughts. Ki squinted up at the bright noon sun. "Jessie, perhaps you'd be more comfortable there under that tree."

Jessica Starbuck's tawny blond hair shimmered golden as she shook her head. "After that long train ride the sun feels rather nice."

"We might be waiting awhile," Ki continued.

"It's not like Scott to be late."

"Just the same, there's no one here."

"Perhaps you'd like to go sit in the shade," she chided him playfully.

He shook his head too. "I'll stay here with you." The matter needed no further discussion.

"What exactly do you know about this man Scott?" he asked abruptly.

"Actually, I don't know all that much," Jessie said with a smile. "Gerald Scott was a friend of my father's. . . ."

Ki nodded. "Your father didn't choose his friends lightly. This Scott must be a good man."

"We've had some business correspondence, but I've never met him," Jessie continued.

Ki looked directly into Jessie's green eyes. "Are we

2

here on Starbuck business or are we helping an old family friend?" he asked coldly.

"Sometimes we make it our business to help friends," Jessie pointed out needlessly.

Ki did not back down. "That doesn't answer my question, Jessie."

"Does it make a difference?" There was the faintest trace of a smile on Jessie's face. She knew it didn't. Ki would support her, and be at her side no matter where she went or what she chose to do.

And Ki knew it too. He started to say "No," then changed his mind. "It's just that I've found favors to be a lot more dangerous than business."

Though she didn't like his ominous tone, Jessie wasn't about to argue. There was much truth in what Ki said. She also knew that Ki's comment was meant to put her on her guard. Ki himself would never shy away from danger; his remark was his way of saying "Let's keep both eyes open."

"Looks like you were right, Jessie," Ki said suddenly as he pointed to a small cloud of dust moving towards them.

"Scott?" Jessie wondered aloud.

"With the exception of a jackrabbit or two we seem to be the only living things hereabouts."

Jessie nodded. "It does seem a long way to go for rabbit," she said with a smile.

She was still smiling when the buckboard pulled to a stop alongside her. But the man driving the wagon was not smiling. "Broke a damn axle!" he exclaimed loudly.

"Mr. Scott?" Jessie inquired.

"I told them to take care of the wash-out and fill in that damned gully. . . . Yep, hop in."

Ki threw their bags into the back of the wagon, then helped Jessie up to the seat. As she sat down next to Scott the man seemed to remember his manners.

Rather sheepishly he removed his Stetson. "Pardon me, Miss Starbuck. I'm a mite ornery; things ain't been going all that well. . . ."

3

"So I gathered from your letter, Mr. Scott."

"I ain't no Mister to Alex Starbuck's daughter," he said with a smile. "Scott'll be just fine."

Jessie returned his smile. "Then call me Jessie, and this is Ki."

Ki was just about to climb into the back, when Scott stopped him. "It can get mighty uncomfortable back there, Ki. I think there's room for all three of us up here." He turned to Jessie. "That is if you don't mind."

"Ki's not just a hired hand," she informed Scott evenly. "Treat him as you would me." Then in a warm tone she added, "And he's the best friend a Starbuck could have."

"Thank you," Ki said.

Scott wasn't sure if Ki had thanked him for the offer of a front seat, or Jessie for the compliment. It didn't matter. He extended his hand to Ki. "That's quite a recommendation." After they shook, Scott flipped the reins and the wagon rolled forward.

Jessie studied the man that sat beside her. He was a bull of a man, as broad as he was tall. With his dark tan and heavily weathered skin, it was hard to guess his age, but Jessie surmised he was well into his fifties. His eyes were dark brown, and wide-set in a face that lacked distinction. It was featureless yet good-looking, with a flat forehead and straight nose. His hands, though, seemed to say the most about the character of the man. They were large, heavily callused, and powerful, but they held the reins ever so gently. Despite the less than gracious introduction, Jessie decided she liked Gerald Scott.

Jessie now turned her attention to the land. At first glance it didn't appear to be the best land for livestock. It was much different from the cattle country of Texas. Instead of a flat, broad expanse of plain, the terrain here was hilly, almost mountainous. The slopes, heavily dotted with white fir, though picturesque, were hardly prime grazing land. But between the forested hammocks cool streams flowed down into the bottomlands. The valleys, even after

4

months of hot summer sun, were a dense, lush green. Somewhat grudgingly, Jessie realized that one of these small sheltered meadows could feed as many head as a hundred acres of prairie.

She turned back to Scott. "When do we reach Double C land?"

"We're already on it," Scott answered with a smile.

"I thought it would be much farther from the depot."

"The ranch is situated so it's a good day's ride to town, but it's only a few hours to the water stop. Our land comes right down to the railroad's right of way," Scott explained.

"Our land?" Ki questioned. "You have partners, Mr. Scott?"

Scott shook his head, and a slow smile crossed his face. "Force of habit, Ki. Ours, meaning Mary's and mine. My wife passed on a few years back."

Ki had started to utter his condolences when the rancher cut him short. "We were together a good spell, an' there weren't no regrets, but lately my heart ain't been in the work, and when a man loafs around he starts gettin' idle thoughts. I sit on the porch and remember the way it used to be, with Mary. Reckon that's one of the reasons I'm puttin' the place up."

"Well Mr. Scott, if we're interested, we'll give you a fair price for it."

"I have no doubts about it, Jessie. That's why I wrote you first."

"I appreciate that," Jessie said sincerely.

"Don't get me wrong, Jessie. I have a heap of respect for you. I hear tell that Alex Starbuck's little girl has become quite a stockman," he said with a grin. "But that's not the only reason I contacted you. The Double C's a large outfit. The largest in these parts. It'll take a good sized bankroll to buy it...."

"I don't think money will be a problem," Jessie began defensively.

Scott cut her short. "That don't need sayin', ma'am. But

5

it'll also take a savvy cattleman to make the investment worthwhile. An' that's why I contacted you, Miss Starbuck. An' you can take that as a compliment."

"I'll do just that," Jessie said, pleased.

"That's why I weren't interested in none of those big eastern syndicates. They's got the money all right, but I don't think they'd be able to turn the Double C around. Like I said, there's been some problems. . . ."

"I haven't seen a problem good ranch hands, a little patience, and a bit of luck can't beat," Jessie said reassuringly.

Scott smiled at her, but didn't answer directly. "I took the liberty of saying my wife's niece is stoppin' over on her way to Frisco."

At first Jessie didn't understand. But then Scott's meaning came through as he continued. "I hope that won't make you too uncomfortable."

"No, I guess not," Jessie started. "But . . ."

"I thought it best if no one knew you came out here to purchase the Double C."

"If you think that was really necessary . . . ?"

"I do," Scott answered plainly. "Not only for me but for you too. As a visitor you might be able to get a better look at the place than as a prospective buyer."

Jessie didn't see the reason in that, and was about to question it further, when Scott snapped the reins and sent the wagon lunging forward.

"Hang on!" he warned, though the advice was unnecessary. Jessie already had a firm grip on the bottom of the wood bench. But even so it was taking all her effort to remain seated. She was thankful for the muscular arm Ki stretched across her lap. She relaxed somewhat as his grip tightened on the seat, securely holding her in place.

"What's wrong?" Jessie had to shout to be heard above the noise of the team and wagon.

"There are some men over the next bluff. An' they

6

don't look like Double C riders," Scott explained as he urged the horses on.

Jessie and Ki exchanged looks. They weren't sure what the unknown riders signified, but they had a pretty good hunch. Jessie wished her Colt were strapped to her side instead of stashed away in her travel sack. She couldn't help but notice that Scott was packing a .44.

As they came over the rise they came practically face to face with the three riders. The wagon couldn't have taken them by surprise; it made too much noise. Yet the men did not flee as she had expected they would.

Scott pulled back hard on the reins, and brought the team to a quick stop.

"You're on my land, Lawry!" As he spoke, Scott's hand went underneath the seat.

Lawry, a short, squat man with a dark, drooping mustache, smiled malevolently at Scott. His teeth were large and tobacco-stained. The other two riders edged their horses off to the side.

Scott seemed unconcerned. "I won't say it again. Off my land!" From underneath the seat his hand emerged holding a Spencer repeating rifle.

Lawry spit tobacco juice and leaned over his saddle horn. "You gonna shoot a man for ridin' yer spread?"

"I'll shoot a man for rustlin' my stock. And I won't think twice about it," Scott answered calmly.

Lawry's face reddened. He straightened in his saddle. He addressed one of his partners, but his eyes remained firm on Scott. "Jake, you reckon I can put two or three slugs into the old wheezer before he even levels that carbine? I'll wager a day's pay I can get three in."

"Why you stinkin' . . ."

Immediately, Jessie placed a hand over Scott's arm. "There may not be a need for that," she said softly.

Lawry let out a laugh. "Looks like yer lady friend's throwing her chips in with me."

7

"I'm doing no such thing," Jessie shot back quickly. "Only before Mr. Scott puts a bullet through your head I'd like to know just what you are doing on Double C land?"

Lawry looked at her with dumbstruck eyes.

"I'll make it easy for you, Mr. Lawry. I don't think you were rustling, or you would have high-tailed it out of here the minute you heard the wagon. What then were you doing, Mister?" When after a moment there was no reply, Jessie turned to Scott. "If he's not talking you might just as well put that bullet in his head." She removed her restraining hand from Scott's arm.

Lawry was once again galvanized into tense alertness. For a moment Jessie wondered if she had made a mistake trying to bluff the man. Maybe he could put a bullet into Scott before the man fired his rifle. Least off he was willing to try. And what of the other two riders? Would they back Lawry? She stole a quick look at them. Their faces held not a clue.

Jessie turned back to Scott. There seemed to be the slightest trace of indecision in his eyes. Jessie suspected it had little to do with fear, and more to do with his inability to draw first. Scott's next words proved her thoughts correct.

"I don't like cutting a man down in cold blood, even the likes of you, Lawry. But if'n you don't turn yer horse around now, we'll bury you where you stand."

Things had come to a head. Scott would waste no more words. On her other side Jessie could feel Ki, tense and ready to spring.

"This is plain loco." It was Jake talking. He turned to Lawry. "I don't give a hoot about the old man, but I'll be damned if I'm gonna let two other folk get all shot up for no damned good reason. And a pretty gal to boot."

"What are you doing on Double C land?" Scott asked Jake. His voice was level, almost relaxed.

"Tell him, Jake," Lawry said. "It ain't no secret."

Jake nodded. "We're lookin' for our own strays. We're

missing a few calves from our southern range; thought they might have wandered over this-a-ways."

Scott seemed unconvinced, but he wasn't going to push any farther. Besides, as Jessie pointed out, if they were intent on rustling they would have hit the breeze. "If we see any sign of them we'll send them over," he said indifferently.

"Much obliged," Jake said as he turned his horse around. The third rider fell in behind him. "Coming, Lawry?"

Lawry, too, turned his horse, but over his shoulder he hurled one more threat at the rancher. "Next time you call me a rustler, old man, I ain't gonna wait for you to draw first."

The Double C ranch house was a good-sized log cabin tucked between rolling hills and a fast-flowing stream. In front of the house, a large corral occupied the center of the valley. Rimmed around it was the bunkhouse; a long, narrow log cabin; a smaller cookhouse; and a big three-storied barn.

The remainder of the ride had passed in silence. It was clear Scott did not want to talk about the incident, and Jessie didn't push. But now as they pulled into the yard, Scott's mood seemed to improve.

"The boys'll be eating dinner now. I usually take my meals up at the house. I expect you'll both join me, but this here's a good time to introduce you around."

Scott stopped the wagon in front of the cookhouse, stepped down, then gave Jessie a hand to the ground. From the cookhouse emerged an elderly Chinese cook. He started a polite bow, but stopped halfway through.

"Hong, this is my niece Jessica, and her friend Ki."

The cook finished his bow, but his eyes were riveted on Ki. Ki sensed and understood the tension that filled the air. The Chinese and Japanese were long-standing enemies. After countless attacks, and years of war, it was no wonder

9

Hong and his people considered Ki's Oriental ancestors as barbaric invaders. But Ki had no wish to perpetuate the image.

"Ching Ho," Ki said sincerely as he gave the cook a deep bow.

Saying nothing, the cook stepped aside and let them enter the cookhouse. It took a moment for Ki to become accustomed to the dark interior, but once he did, his eyes grew even wider with shock and amazement. He hardly heard a word Scott said. Sitting down at two long tables were the crew of the Double C. There were at least twenty hungry cowboys, and they all turned to stare at him. Forty slanted eyes filled with surprise and hatred. The crew of the Double C were all Chinese.

Still in a daze, Ki carried their bags into the ranch house, where the second surprise, by the name of Ling Ling, took him unawares.

"This is my housekeeper, Ling Ling," Scott said off-handedly. "Show Jessie and Ki to their rooms," he said to the young Chinese woman. "Then set the table for two more."

Fascinated, Ki stared at Ling Ling. There was no denying that she was beautiful. She had soft, creamy skin the color of fresh churned butter. Her long, straight hair, though tied back in a braid, glistened with a healthy shine, and her eyes were the gentlest, softest earth-brown he had ever seen. But there was something more; something that could only be called captivating.

"Ki, this way." Her soft voice cut through the fog in Ki's head.

Apparently he had been staring, dumbstruck. Her mouth was small and puckered with fleshy red lips. . . . He would have given anything to see her smile. . . . Speechless, he followed her.

The house, surprisingly, was similar to a Texas house. The large main cabin was the dining room, parlor, and kitchen. Tacked on behind that was a smaller room that Ki

10

took to be Scott's. Off to the right was a smaller guest cabin comprised of two bedrooms. The dogtrot, the covered passageway between the main house and the guest cabin, was piled high with stacked wood.

They showed Jessie to her room first. Ki placed Jessie's bag on her bed, then followed Ling Ling to his room, the second and last door down the hall.

"I'll bring some hot water for you to wash in," she said as she turned to leave. But then she stopped. "Why do you stare at me like that?" she asked abruptly.

Because you are so beautiful, Ki wanted to say. But instead he shook his head slowly. "I don't know," was all he could manage.

All that night he lay in bed and wondered about Ling Ling. But not in the way a man would usually wonder about a woman. Not who she was and where she was or what she was doing. Not how to court her or make her happy. He simply wondered why he was so taken with her. Her beauty alone could not explain it. He had been with equally ravishing women, who had not had nearly the effect this little Chinese housekeeper was having on him. He shook his head, trying to clear it. Her looks alone could not account for the shortness of his breath or the tightening of his heart. But the more he thought about it the less sense it made, and the stonger grew the discomfort in the pit of his stomach.

Eventually he drifted off into a fitful sleep, where he was haunted by visions of slanting eyes—eyes filled with hatred. But one pair stood out, warm and compassionate.

Ki awoke with a start, his body covered in a cold sweat. He rolled over onto his back, and for a moment stared up at the ceiling before crossing his hands over his chest. He took slow, deliberate breaths, deeply inhaling, then fully exhaling. One after another. . . .

Chapter 2

There were a hundred candles flickering. Incense sticks sent up curls of fragrant smoke. The walls glistened gold. Soft chanting lured him in deeper. A warm glow filled his spirit. It was a temple—a Buddhist shrine.

And Ki was suddenly plucked from this haven.

The tap at the door came again, and then a soft voice: "Breakfast is on the table."

He woke up slowly, sadness filling his heart as the present reality of the ranch house replaced the reality of his dream.

"Hurry up, Ki. Eggs get cold quickly."

A slow smile crossed his face. It wasn't the thought of eggs, but Ling Ling's beckoning voice that cheered him.

Ki said good morning to Jessie and Scott and sat himself

down in front of a plate filled with eggs, biscuits, and sliced ham. He had taken only a few bites when a Chinese ranch hand knocked on the door and entered the room.

"Charlie and Wo are back from the line camp," the cowboy began.

"Jessie, Ki—this is Tsen-ti, my foreman," Scott said by way of introduction. "A rancher would be hard pressed to find a better hand."

Tsen-ti ignored the two visitors and continued excitedly. "They spotted some sign of cattle heading off towards the Lazy M."

"And . . ." Scott prompted.

"They followed the tracks, but only far enough to be sure the critters weren't on the other side of the break."

Scott nodded. "Good. I don't want any of my men risking danger alone. When we go after rustlers we'll take half the outfit."

"It's possible they just strayed," Tsen-ti said cautiously.

"Did they?" Scott wanted to know.

The foreman shrugged. "I'd have to take a look for myself before I said. Wo ain't that good at reading sign."

"Take six men with you and go have a look." When the foreman left, Scott turned to Jessie. "I should have shot that Lawry dead when I had the chance."

"Maybe we should tag along with Tsen-ti," Jessie suggested. "I wouldn't mind getting a look at the ranch."

Scott hesitated a moment. "I rather you didn't. If there was any rough play . . ."

Jessie smiled. "I'm not a stranger to gunplay, Scott. I do run the Circle Star, and not from behind a desk either."

"But that's your own spread, Jessie. Here you're my guest." Jessie started to speak, but Scott cut her off. "I'd never forgive myself if you were to get hurt. And that's the end of it. I'll show you and Ki around the spread myself."

"We don't want to put you to any trouble," Jessie protested gently. "I'm sure there are more important things for you to be doing."

"There's nothing as pressing as seeing to your needs, Jessie."

"Now, with an outfit this size that just can't be true."

Scott smiled. "There's always some damned paperwork I keep putting off."

"Ki and I can have a look around for ourselves."

"Well, if that suits you, there are some tally sheets that need my attention."

"Good. Then you get to them, and if we can impose upon you for a pair of saddle horses . . ."

"Of course. I'll have two horses brought around to the house."

"Don't put yourself to the trouble," Jessie said as she stood up from the table. "We'll go down and fetch them ourselves."

"All right. Tommy's a good boy. He's Ling Ling's nephew, and he'll set you up fine. Then go round the cookhouse and have Hong pack you a lunch sack," Scott added as an afterthought.

"We'll do that," Ki said as he too got up from the table.

"Uh, Ki, I don't mean nothing by this, and I sure hope you don't take this wrong, but if you'll be needing a gun, there are extras locked in the parlor cabinet."

"Thank you, but that won't be necessary," Ki replied.

"Jessie, I don't mean to tell you your business," Scott continued, "but perhaps it would be best if you went travelin' with some sort of protection."

"I couldn't agree more. That's why I take Ki with me."

"But you should have some firepower behind you. Like I said, Ki should feel free to help himself to any gun he'd—"

Jessie was smiling broadly. "Ki doesn't have a need for guns, Scott, and if you're worried about me—"

"I am."

"—I pack my own custom-made Colt .38. It has a beautiful peachwood handle. A little small for a man's hand, but perfect for mine."

Scott let out a laugh. "I really shouldn't worry about you, should I? You are your father's daughter."

With a wink, Jessie turned and left the house. Ki followed behind.

As they walked to the barn, Jessie turned to Ki. "While I get the horses, why don't you pick up our lunch?"

"I don't think that's a wise decision, Jessie."

"It'll be a long day. We'll have to have something to eat," she protested gently.

"That's not quite what I meant," Ki answered with a smile. "How about if I get the horses and you get the lunch?"

Jessie shook her head. "I wanted to have a look at the horses. You can tell a lot about an outfit by the mounts they ride."

"Good idea."

"Then I'm sure to have worked up a whopping hunger," Jessie added with a smile. It had become something of a game between them now.

"Never hurt a man, or a woman for that matter, to go without a meal every now and then."

"Why Ki," Jessie snapped. "If you're implying what I think you are . . ."

Ki backed off momentarily. "All I'm saying is I don't want to go to Hong to pick up lunch." Then he grinned slyly. "But if the shoe fits, wear it."

"It's not my shoe size I'm worried about!"

Ki feigned ignorance. "Is your head getting bigger than your hat?" He looked at her closely. "That doesn't seem to be."

He had barely finished his words when Jessie whipped off her Stetson and whacked him over the head with it. She was about to strike again, but Ki had already skipped out beyond her arm's length.

"When I think of all those quiet, inscrutable Chinese, and I have to wind up with a loudmouthed, wisecracking Jap— Why that's it, isn't it, Ki? You don't like Hong because he's Chinese!" Very self-satisfied, Jessie returned the Stetson to the top of her head.

"All I said was, I didn't think I'd be hungry."

"But it's true just the same, isn't it?"

Ki shook his head.

"Ki . . ." she started to reprimand.

"More accurately, Hong and the others don't like me."

"Because you're Japanese." It was not a question.

Ki nodded and briefly explained the centuries of conflict between the two neighboring peoples.

Jessie listened with interest. But when Ki finished, there was a puzzled look on her face. "It doesn't make sense. You and Hong have so much in common."

Ki disagreed.

"You're both Oriental," Jessie blurted out.

Ki let out a laugh. "And all Indians are red brothers."

"They are," Jessie began emphatically, but then quieted down. "But I see what you mean, Ki."

Ki nodded. "The Tonkawas and the Comanche are always going to be bitter enemies. Nothing will change that."

"But the Chinese and Japanese? Must it be the same?" Jessie wondered out loud.

Ki didn't answer.

They had reached the barn, and for the moment the topic was dropped. Tommy, as predicted, was a friendly and eager Chinese boy, with a round face, short black bangs, and bright brown eyes. Discreetly, Jessie studied how Tommy interacted with Ki. She could detect no overt hatred, and took the boy's age to be the reason for that. From his speech it was easy to guess that Tommy had spent most, if not all, of his thirteen years in America and would have had little reason to harbor resentment for the Japanese. About the only emotion Jessie saw in the boy was a strong hankering to be out on the range with the other hands.

Tommy showed them the horses, describing in detail the

16

temperament and strong points of each animal. Jessie was impressed, not only with the stable boy's knowledge and interest, but with the wide variety of horses in the stable. The perfect horse, though talked about by many, was mostly a myth of the range. The qualities necessary for the "perfect horse" were often mutually exclusive of each other.

A perfect horse would be big and strong, yet not tire easily, even after a full day's ride. He would have a good disposition, but have enough fire in him to take to a chase. And he would be quick and nimble, yet have strong legs and ankles to resist injury.

Perhaps ranching best showed up the problems inherent in finding a "perfect horse." It was every rancher's dream to have a mount that could outrun a calf, but that possessed the strength to topple a bull, and could do both hour after hour without tiring.

Every cowboy had a favorite horse story, telling how his prized animal pulled a fully loaded wagon out of a mud bog, or worked all day, non-stop, rounding up stray calves. The tales were endless, but all amounted to the same thing.

Yet an animal that had one accomplished skill did not make a perfect horse. The size and strength that enabled one horse to pull a wagon also kept him from running all day delivering mailbags. And the horse that was quick and nimble did not have the bulk to control a full-grown steer at the end of a rope. Horses just couldn't be expected to perform every task with equal proficiency. And every good cowboy knew that. That's why they had different horses for different jobs. It was a mark of a good outfit that their barn was stocked with a varying assortment of horses. Tommy pointed out the strong work animals, the quick cutting horses, and the smart roping steeds.

"This here is Smoke," Tommy announced when they came to a large gray mare. "She's an awful gentle critter, and I don't suppose she'll give you much trouble, Miss Jessie."

"She's a pretty one," Jessie noted as she stroked the horse's neck.

"I'll get you a saddle from the tack room. I don't know if we have one your size, but I'll grab the smallest one I can find."

"Don't worry about that, Tommy. I'll manage all right," Jessie assured him.

Tommy nodded. "Just remember to keep your feet in the stirrups, and you'll be fine," Tommy advised.

"Anything else?" Jessie asked with a twinkle in her eye. That Tommy naturally assumed she was a novice rider rather amused her.

"And don't ever let go of the reins."

"Okay," Jessie said making a mental note of the instructions.

"And don't be afraid to hang on to the saddle horn. Just don't let the reins drop."

"I'll try and remember," Jessie said in all seriousness. Tommy left to get a saddle, and Jessie whispered in the horse's ear. "Well, Smoke, what say we play a little prank on Tommy?"

Ki didn't have to hear Jessie to know what she was thinking. "Jessie, I wouldn't. Just because Tommy says she's gentle is no indication that—"

"Hush up," Jessie said softly.

Ki persisted. When it involved Jessie's safety Ki would have his say. "Gentle as she may be, you're still a stranger to her, and there's no telling how she'll react."

Jessie's mind was made up. "Look at those eyes, Ki. Not only is she gentle but she has a real sense of humor."

"Well I'm not one to argue with your horse sense, Jessie."

"Good."

"And besides, I could use a good laugh."

Without another word, Jessie wrapped her arms around the horse's neck, then swung herself up onto the animal's

18

back. Smoke twitched her ears and gave her head a quick shake, but it was more a sign of curiosity than annoyance. Jessie settled her weight, then turned to Ki. "If you wouldn't mind?" she said politely, as she gestured to the stall door.

"Certainly." Ki opened the door, and Smoke pranced out of the barn.

A moment later Tommy returned, carrying a heavy saddle. "Hey, what happened? Where's Smoke?"

"Have a look for yourself," Ki said with a tilt of the head.

Still carrying the saddle, Tommy followed Ki to the barn door.

Outside, Jessie and Smoke were gliding around the corral. Without the aid of a saddle or bridle, Jessie was forced to conform to every movement of the animal. A naturally smooth rider, Jessie looked even more graceful without the encumbrance of the saddle. With her arms wrapped low around the horse's neck and her body pressing down against the animal, Jessie's body seemed to melt into the sleek back of the gray mare. So smooth were the two that it was difficult to tell where animal ended and rider began.

Tommy could only utter one word: "Gosh."

At the far end of the corral, Jessie turned and, with a wave, came charging back. At first Tommy wasn't sure of Jessie's intentions, but they soon became clear, and his jaw dropped. It remained open as Smoke and Jessie vaulted the corral fence and went sailing though the air.

Jessie brought the gray mare to a stop before the awe-struck boy. "You're right, Tommy," she said with a smile. "She is a gentle horse."

"Gosh," the boy repeated. "I ain't ever seen anyone ride like that."

"I'll take that as a compliment."

"How'd you ever learn to do that, Miss Jessie?" the boy asked eagerly.

19

Jessie smiled. "I grew up on a ranch," she stated simply.

"Gosh. I grew up on a ranch too, but I can't do that."

Jessie showed sudden interest. "Did you grow up on the Double C?"

Tommy nodded. "Mostly."

"Where were you before?"

"Chinatown. I came here with my aunt."

Now Ki showed a sudden interest in the conversation. "Ling Ling was with you in San Francisco?"

Tommy nodded, but clearly he was not interested in discussing his background. He was still taken by Jessie's riding. Tommy kicked at the saddle that lay at his feet. "Guess you don't have much of a need for this."

"Don't be silly," Jessie said with a grin. "A gal's got to have a place to tie her rope."

Instantly, Tommy turned and ran into the barn. He returned a moment later carrying a coiled lasso. "Could you show me some roping?"

Jessie slid down from her horse and took the lasso from Tommy. With her other hand she pulled Tommy to her, and quickly wrapped the rope around him.

"That's not what I meant," Tommy squealed between peals of laughter.

"You have some horses to saddle up, young man, and we have some riding to do. But later I don't see why we can't take you and your horse out for some roping practice."

"I don't have a horse of my own yet, ma'am," Tommy said with lowered eyes. "But Uncle says if I take good care of the barn, he'll rope me a wild mustang this summer."

"Well you better do a good job, and heed your uncle," Jessie said. "Because you'll want your own horse under you when you start working the spring roundup."

"Yes, ma'am," the boy replied. As he ran back to the barn, it was obvious Jessie had made a new friend.

A few minutes later, Jessie sat tall in the saddle. Alongside her, Ki was mounted on a smaller roan.

"Now about that lunch . . ." Jessie began with a smile.

"Well, now that you're in the saddle I can see those new Levi's seem to fit you just fine, Jessie. . . ."

"I do believe you're trying to flatter me, Ki."

"Nope, just thinking I might be a bit hungry come lunchtime."

"What happened to the benefits of skipping a meal here and there?" Jessie asked with mock interest.

"I don't think two active people have to worry much about excess weight."

"Oh?" Jessie's eyebrows went up. "Now you're outright calling me fat?"

Ki squirmed. "I'm doing nothing of the sort, Jessie. I meant we don't have to worry about getting fat."

Jessie was smiling. "I know just what you meant, Ki. I'll go and ask Hong to pack us some food." She nudged her horse towards the cookhouse. "When you finally get your foot out of your mouth it'll be time for lunch."

Leaving the barn, they headed almost due north. They passed through the same territory as they had the day they arrived, but on horseback they weren't restricted only to the wagon road.

They threaded their way among the many foothills that ran through the Double C, coming eventually to a large meadow. Jessie stopped her horse and turned to Ki. "Why don't we head off here? I'd like to see what the grazing is beyond that ridge."

Ki looked down at the dirt, then smiled at Jessie. "I'm sure your curiosity has nothing to do with the fact that the Double C riders also turned off here."

"I hadn't noticed. What a coincidence." Jessie managed to say it with a straight face, but Ki wasn't fooled.

"What do you expect to find, Jessie?"

"Cowpunchers doing their job?"

"What else?" Ki asked slyly.

Jessie shrugged her shoulders. "Nothing really. If anything, I'm just curious to see Chinese cowpokes in action."

Ki looked disappointed. "I thought you had suspicions."

"I leave those to you, Ki," Jessie said with a smile.

Ki returned the smile. "I just thought you were developing the hang of it."

Jessie shook her head. "Why bother? You're too good at it."

"It never hurts to be on your guard," Ki warned seriously.

Jessie wanted to tell Ki to stop worrying and let her be, but she restrained her impulse. Ki's extra-cautious attitude had saved them from trouble more than once.

Though it was well into the morning, the sun was still behind the eastern hill. Light was filtering through the pine trees, dotting the meadow with patches of sun and shade. As the breeze blew through the trees, the carpet of grass shimmered and danced in changing patterns. By late afternoon, with the sun high in the sky, the temperature would rise twenty degrees. But now the meadow had a cool, fresh smell.

It hardly seemed the time or place to worry about danger, Jessie thought to herself. But that was the thing of it. Danger could never be predicted. Not totally. One knew when one was going into a dangerous situation, but the precise moment when danger would strike was always a mystery. Oh, Jessie had seen Ki react to situations as if he had a second sense about him, but what others viewed as a close kin to magic, Jessie knew to be skill, training, and acute senses. It wasn't that Ki knew when the wolf would strike; it was just that he would hear the birds take flight, and be forewarned. Or he would hear the whinny of a horse or the crack of a branch. If one were attuned and listening, there was always a warning. That was why Ki was forever telling Jessie to be on her guard. But then again, Ki was sometimes taken by surprise. He'd even been knocked unconscious by a man hiding behind a door.

22

It didn't happen often, but it did happen. And that just reinforced Ki's warning that danger could strike at any time.

A thought struck Jessie. "I'm surprised there are no cattle grazing here."

"I was wondering the same thing myself," Ki replied. "The meadow is almost ideal—green and close to home."

"When we get back I'll ask Scott about it."

But in another half a mile, there was no need for that. They came upon a large watering hole and their question was answered. The painted sign boldly displaying a crudely drawn skull and crossbones was hardly necessary. One look at the dry, bleached skeleton of what looked like a deer was enough for Jessie to know the water hole had gone bad.

"Well there's our answer, Ki." She turned her horse away from the hole, and continued past. As a rancher, the sight of bad water always put Jessie ill at ease.

"I'm not so sure."

"Ki, I wouldn't graze my herds within a few miles of alkalied water. I doubt Scott would either."

A smile crossed Ki's face. "You're making an assumption, Jessie. That's—"

"Of course I am." Jessie shot back quickly. "I'm assuming Scott is a rational man, and an intelligent rancher."

"I don't doubt that." Ki was still smiling. "But your assumption about the alkalied water is incorrect."

"Well that makes three of us then," Jessie said sarcastically. "Me, the man who posted that sign, and the deer who drank from the water. I suppose we're all mistaken, and there's absolutely nothing wrong with that water."

Ki shook his head. "I'm not saying that, Jessie."

Jessie was hardly listening. She continued angrily, "I'm sure the sign is somebody's idea of a practical joke, and the animal just happened to die of old age a few feet from the water hole."

Ki let out a laugh. "I don't think you'd convince me."

His laugh and his comment left Jessie confused, and she admitted it. "Then just what are you getting at, Ki?"

"You made a natural assumption," Ki began patiently, "based on your experience with the Circle Star, and for that matter most of Texas, and the prairie, clear up to the Rockies—"

"And what was that?" Jessie asked impatiently.

"The alkali. I won't say positively without getting a geologist out here, but this is not alkalied soil. In more arid land, the alkali will sometimes naturally seep from the soil into the water. . . ."

Jessie nodded her head, as she began to understand what Ki was getting at. "It happens in the Panhandle all the time."

"That's why it was natural for you to assume the water turned alkalied. But look at those hills." Ki pointed to the slope that lay behind the water hole. "There's the watershed. That slope's covered with pine. If anything the soil is a bit acidic. The pond would be hard water all right, but a few minerals never killed a thing."

Jessie was quick to pick up the ramifications of Ki's observation. "But then you're saying somebody poisoned the hole."

"I'm not saying that exactly, but there is a strong probability of it."

"Would Scott have made the same mistake I made?" Jessie wondered aloud. "Would he jump to the conclusion the water naturally turned alkalied?"

Ki shrugged his shoulders.

Jessie broke into a grin. "I reckon you can't answer that, can you, Ki?"

"Now before you start thinking sabotage, Jessie, there might be a very good reason we are not aware of that caused the water to turn bad."

"There might be," Jessie responded, but she seemed unconvinced. After a moment, she turned back to Ki. "What do you think?"

"I think it's a question we'll have to put to Scott."

Though Ki didn't come right out and say it, his noncommittal answer told Jessie he had his suspicions.

There wasn't much time to ponder, though, before they heard the first shot ring out.

★

Chapter 3

Jessie spurred her horse into a gallop and took off in the direction of the shot. But in the few seconds that had elapsed, the single shot had multiplied, and now gunshots were being fired nonstop. Jessie slowed her horse to a trot; she had no desire to run full speed into a blazing gunfight.

A moment later, Ki pulled up alongside her. "I'm glad you slowed down, Jessie. It might be wiser to assess the situation first."

"You won't get an argument from me."

Ki pointed up ahead to where two slopes pinched the meadow into a narrow pass. "It sounds like the shots are coming from the far end of that canyon."

Jessie agreed. "If we cut across that hill, we might even sneak up on the shooting match."

It took a few minutes to wind their way up the forested

incline. Though they could have moved quicker and taken a more direct route, Jessie and Ki chose to stick to the cover of the trees. They didn't know what they would come across and wanted to be certain they wouldn't inadvertently wander into someone's gunsight.

When they reached the ridge, the situation became plain. "Looks like we were careful for nothing," Jessie said with a sigh.

Ki wasn't so discouraged. "There was a fifty-fifty chance we'd come upon the gunmen. We just chose the wrong hill."

Below them, at the base of the hill, the Double C crew were taking refuge behind any available cover. On the opposite slope the crack of rifle fire kept the Chinese pinned down. But periodically one of the Chinese would stick his arm out from behind a rock or tree trunk and fire a shot across the field. Even if the ranch hands had taken the time to sight, the riflemen on the slope were almost out of range. A wild shot aimed somewhere at the hill was just a gesture, and a futile one at that.

Ki felt the same. "They might just as well save their ammunition," he noted dryly.

"Maybe they're covering for a flanker."

"It's a possibility."

"It's the only thing that makes sense. Send a man around to outflank the ambushers."

"A good idea. But they're not doing it," Ki announced.

"How can you tell?"

"Six men left the Double C; there were six sets of prints. . . ."

"Right . . ."

"Now count them."

From their vantage point it was not difficult to spot the Double C hands. It only took Jessie a few seconds. "Six of them," she said defeatedly. "Then it's up to us to save them," she added.

"I'd like to figure out what happened."

"Let's help them first, then put the pieces together later. How many gunmen on that hill?"

"I can't get a clear look at any," Ki admitted. "But from the rifle smoke I only count two, maybe three."

"I thought three, but one could be constantly on the move. For argument's sake, let's assume three."

"Doesn't make much difference, Jessie; two or three, we can't go charging the hill. They'd cut us down before we got halfway there."

"Then we'll outflank them. We still have the element of surprise."

"I'm not so sure about that either." Ki pointed to the top of the ridge. "In the thicket just to the right of that forked tree . . ."

With Ki's help Jessie spotted the horse that was tethered to the bushes. "You think it's a lookout?"

Ki nodded. "There could be a man up there guarding their flank, or it could have been a lookout that spotted us way across the meadow. Either way the odds are against us."

"But if we don't do something the odds are definitely against them," she said gesturing to the Chinese.

"I'm not even sure about that."

"I am," Jessie snapped, but she softened her tone and started to ask Ki why he thought that.

"Look!" Ki interrupted.

In the distance, Jessie saw a large brown mass against the green grass. "Cattle!" she exclaimed excitedly. "With that bad water hole back there, they must be strays." She thought a moment, then added, "Or rustled."

"Could be," Ki noted. "Judging from what's going on down there, I wouldn't be too surprised."

"Right now, it doesn't matter," Jessie said with a smile. "That herd has just given me an idea."

Ki was aware of the possibilities. "If you're thinking of stampeding them—"

"Why not?"

"It won't be easy to get them to run headlong into a gunfight."

"If we can make more ruckus behind them they won't know where they're heading, and they won't care. One Colt, at close range, will make a heck of a lot more noise than all that shooting down there."

Ki didn't seem convinced. "But there's only one gun. We'll never get the herd to make the turn down the pass."

Jessie also realized the flaw in the plan. With only her gun to spook them the herd could turn in any direction. It would be unlikely that they would run back towards the gunfire that was going on at the base of the slope. Ki could try turning them by waving his arms, but more than likely, with Jessie spooking them with her pistol, Ki would get trampled by the frightened animals.

Suddenly Ki brightened. "But there is your whole gun-belt of cartridges. I think it might work."

"How?"

"Let's get over there first. Then I'll explain."

Jessie started to speak, but Ki cut her off. "The quicker we get there, the sooner we can get those men out of danger."

Up close the Herefords were broader and not as lanky as longhorns. From afar, Jessie guessed there were upwards of seventy head in the herd, but now she realized there might be closer to a hundred.

For resistance to disease and strength of survival, the Texas longhorn couldn't be beat. But looking at these massive animals, Jessie began to wonder about crossbreeding. The longhorn did well on the skimpy grass of the prairie, but Jessie suspected that in order to thrive, these hefty animals needed lots and lots of feed.

Jessie approached one of the cows slowly. She wasn't sure of the temperament of the animal and didn't want to startle it, at least not prematurely. But her worries were for nothing. The she-thing raised her big white head and stared vacantly at Jessie. Apparently the animal's only concern was chewing her cud.

"Kind of silly looking, aren't they?" Jessie said as she looked into the Hereford's large brown eyes.

"All the white faces?"

Jessie nodded.

"Gives them a rather unintelligent look, I'd say," Ki continued.

"Oh no," Jessie softly cooed, as if to assuage the insult. "I'd say it's a gentle, peaceful look," she added, as if the animal could understand.

"Let's hope it's not too gentle—and that it spooks easily, or our plan won't work."

Jessie laid aside thoughts of cattle breeding and turned back to the more pressing problem of the present. "Now what do you want me to do?" she asked Ki.

"First give me your gunbelt," he said as he dismounted. "Then go round up whatever firewood you can."

Jessie slipped down from the saddle, unstrapped her gunbelt, and handed it to Ki.

"I don't need all that much wood, just enough to start a few brush fires."

"I won't be long," Jessie promised, then hurried off to collect the wood.

Meanwhile Ki reached into his pocket and pulled out one of his *shuriken*. The silver throwing stars were not only an effective and lethal weapon, but a handy tool as well. He cut a swatch from his saddle blanket, then took a dozen bullets from the gun belt and laid them on the ground. Using the sharp edge of the throwing stars, he dug into the soft lead of the bullets and pried them off of the cartridges, being careful not to spill any of the gunpowder. He then ripped a small piece of the blanket and stuffed it into the open end of the cartridge. He was just stuffing the last shell when Jessie came up carrying a large bundle of wood.

"I've another pile gathered over there," Jessie began.

"I think this will be enough."

Jessie looked puzzled. "There's hardly enough wood here to frighten one animal. To start a blaze that'll turn a whole herd we'll need ten times this."

"No we won't," Ki said with a smile. "If I intended to scare them with a brush fire you'd be correct. But there's something much better than that." He held out his hand and showed Jessie the modified cartridges. "Courtesy of the Chinese."

Jessie understood what Ki was doing, but didn't understand his reference. "Why the Chinese?"

"They invented the firecracker," Ki explained, as he handed back her gunbelt.

"Then it's only fitting that it help them out of a jam. Too bad I'm not toting my old Remington anymore. It would have made your job a lot easier."

The Remington was a cap and ball revolver. The gun was loaded with loose powder and a ball and a percussion cap instead of a ready-made cartridge.

Ki smiled. "It would also be a lot more fun."

"A lot louder, too," Jessie added.

"That's what I said, more fun." Ki repeated with a grin.

"Ki, sometimes I think you're still a kid at heart," Jessie proclaimed.

With a playful shrug, Ki shoved the cartridges into his vest pocket, and went off to set up the fires.

He returned a few minutes later. "I set the wood up in three piles. That should do it," he said as he mounted his horse. "When I wave my arms, you start them in my direction."

Jessie nodded. "Be careful, Ki."

"You too, Jessie," Ki said. Then he urged his horse into a trot. Over his shoulder he called out a final caution. "Once they're moving into the pass, back off."

While Ki got ready, doubt began to haunt Jessie, the same doubt that must have impelled Ki to issue that final warning. Jessie was well aware that a stampeding herd was

31

anything but controllable. Ideally, she would like to run the herd up the slope and rout out the ambushers, but that might be more wishful thinking than reality. But if they just manuevered the cattle into the pass, the thundering herd would kick up enough dust to give the Double C hands enough cover to ride out of the ambush. But the fact that the Double C workers themselves would be momentarily in the path of the stampeding animals gave her concern. If the Chinese panicked, or if their horses balked, they would be in a more dangerous situation than just being pinned down by rifle fire. They could be trampled underfoot.

It was a risk, but it was a risk they would have to take. It offered them a chance, and a good one at that. As things stood, they would eventually fall prey to the ambushers' rifles. This way they had a chance.

Jessie caught herself quickly. She had to stop thinking of the trapped men as "Chinese." Despite herself, the tag carried with it a certain helplessness, at least with things American. Yes, the men trapped in the pass were Chinese, but they were not Chinese cooks and coolies. They were ranch hands. If it were her men, Circle Star men, trapped in there, she would have had confidence in their abilities to handle themselves correctly and get to safety. The Chinese in there were Double C riders. To a seasoned trail driver stampedes were par for the course. On his first drive, a cowpoke learned quickly how to deal with frightened herds, or he didn't get a second chance. Again she reminded herself that these men were hands hired by a seasoned rancher. If Scott hired them, she would trust his judgment.

Then she saw Ki waving his hat. There was no more time to ruminate. She only hoped Scott's judgment was sound.

She slipped her Colt from its holster, and with a lively whoop fired the gun into the air.

The cattle were slow to react. Jessie had to bear down on them and fire two more shots before she really had them

32

on the run. But once moving the herd bunched up and stayed together.

At his end, Ki waited patiently. The three fires, roughly twenty-five yards apart, were all crackling hotly. The metal "firecrackers" were cool in his hand. He eased back in his saddle. There was nothing to do but wait for the herd to thunder towards him.

It took Ki a minute to realize the herd was already in motion. The mass of cattle was heading towards him straight on, and their movement was hard to detect. Also, on the thick, green grass, little dust was kicked up.

Ki sensed the tremor at almost the same time his eyes perceived the movement. Under him his horse fidgeted nervously. Ki reached over and stroked his neck. "Keep calm," he whispered soothingly. Ki knew there was a possibility of failure. In theory everything would work fine. But a hundred head of frightened cattle could never be relied upon to fit into theory. Too many things could go wrong. Ki had calculated his part carefully, or so he thought. But now a glaring error showed itself.

His horse was an unknown. Ki had no idea how it would react to the stampede. Ki had assumed the horse would perform like a Circle Star animal. But that was a big assumption to make. It was one thing for a horse to ride herd on a stampede; it was another thing for it to stand steadfastly in the path of oncoming death. In the face of the thundering herd, the horse might panic. If Ki couldn't control his mount, he would never be able to change the path of the stampede. And if he couldn't turn the herd, they would never get them into the pass, and the plan would do nothing to help free the trapped Chinese. But that was a minor problem. If Ki couldn't turn the herd, the mass of cattle would continue—straight towards him. . . .

Jessie kept her horse close to the heels of the last cow. The herd was moving well. They weren't as edgy or as quick to run as longhorns, but they were stampedeing just the same. Periodically an animal would lag behind. At first

Jessie scared them back into the stampede, but she decided a few dropouts hardly mattered, as long as the leaders kept running, and the centers continued to push.

Jessie looked to her right. The pass was coming in view. Any time now the herd should start turning. She hoped Ki wasn't going to wait till the last minute. Then she looked ahead just in time to see Ki's mount rearing up wildly.

The horse was nearly vertical, fully extended on its hind legs. Miraculously, skillfully, Ki hung in the saddle. One arm waved above his head. The other hand, Jessie knew, would be locked tightly into the horse's mane—not only to help Ki stay mounted, but most importantly to keep the animal's head up. With a head held erect, the ability of a horse to buck was lessened.

For the longest instant time seemed to stand still. Like a statue, the horse hung in the air, with Ki, perfectly still, silhouetted against the clear blue sky. Then the world collapsed.

The horse went down, toppling on its side.

Jessie let out a scream and spurred her horse forward. But there was nothing she could do. She couldn't part the mass of cattle flesh and go galloping through the herd to rescue Ki. Even if she could get through the crush, the leaders would have reached Ki first. The same went for riding around the side. She just didn't have enough time.

There was nothing she could do but wait and hope. Frustration was tearing away at her; Ki was in trouble and there was nothing she could do to save him. But it was her comprehension of the situation that wrenched at her heart. She hoped with all her soul, but she knew the chance of Ki surviving was slim.

The fall could have knocked him unconscious, or his leg could have been shattered by the weight of the horse. Ki would be lying on the ground, defenseless and unprotected. Jessie also knew that occasionally a herd on the run would seperate and avoid an object lying in their path. But it would take only one errant hoof to smash Ki's skull.

There was a chance, but Jessie feared that more likely than not Ki's body would soon be nothing more than lifeless, pulverized flesh.

Helplessly she waited, hoping that the horse would gain its feet, and that Ki would still be in the saddle. But even that faint hope was crushed. Jessie saw the horse rise and run off, but Ki was not to be seen.

No doubt Ki was lying face down waiting for 400 hooves—more than twenty-five tons—to pound him into the ground.

Chapter 4

The herd was thundering closer. The horse wanted to bolt. It was shifting uneasily from side to side, but Ki kept tight hold on the reins. They had to wait for the proper moment.

Ki felt the horse stiffen. Quickly, he pressed his muscular thighs hard against the sides of the animal. The horse was going to buck, that was certain. But Ki didn't know in which direction. He kept his torso loose and flexible, ready to lean in any direction.

But when the horse reared straight up, Ki was taken by surprise. Only his strength and superb balance kept him astride. If the animal came down kicking, Ki didn't expect to hang on long. He had to calm the animal and get him under control quickly.

He grabbed hold of the roan's mane. For a moment they seemed suspended in space, but then the frightened animal lost its balance. It had overextended itself and couldn't support its own weight and that of its rider. It started to fall.

Ki slid his feet from the stirrups. If the horse went over on its side the last thing Ki wanted was to be pinned under it. If he managed to stay in the saddle, the horse might regain its feet, and only seconds would be lost. But there was a high probability of serious injury, either to Ki or the horse. On foot he would have less of a chance against the stampede, but if he let himself get thrown from the horse now there was a good chance he'd escape injury. There was little time to think, but Ki was certain he'd rather face the charging cattle uninjured. He relaxed his body and let go of the horse. . . .

He was almost parallel to the ground when he felt himself thrown free from the saddle. He hit the ground hard, but the grass softened the blow. With a quick roll Ki was on his feet.

The cattle were almost upon him. He could flatten himself to the ground and hope for the best, but that was out of his character. As long as there was a chance, he'd rather go down fighting. He had no hope of outrunning the herd, at least not with the nearest tree a hundred yards away. But there was one chance left to him, if the cartridges hadn't slipped out in his fall. . . . He dug his hand into his vest pocket. His fingers curled around the smooth metal of his "firecrackers."

There was the faintest smile on his lips as he raced to the first of his fires. If he could outrun the herd . . . And if the "firecrackers" didn't take too long to explode . . .

The pounding hooves caused the ground to quake. He could hear the heavy breathing, the powerful grunts, as the animals barrelled down on him. He imagined he could feel the moisture of their spittle on the back of his neck. He dared not turn around.

His legs pumped faster. He took longer strides. Each foot barely touched down before it was swinging up and out again. His whole body worked in unison. His arms clawed the air, helping to propel him faster. His mouth gaped open, sucking in as much air as possible. This was an all-out effort. It had to be a hundred percent, or nothing.

He could smell the fear of the animals, enveloping him in a thick cloud. He could see the fire just ahead.

From three yards away he tossed the cartridges into the flames. Almost instantly he heard the first of the explosions. The second sharp crack followed soon after. The next two firecrackers went off with a thundering boom, exploding almost as one.

He didn't slow down, but continued his mad dash for the next fire. However, he did steal a quick glance over his shoulder.

The herd was turning! It amazed Ki how fast a quarter ton of flesh, bone, and muscle could change direction. Fear was a powerful force and a potent motivator. He smiled to himself. He didn't think he had ever run so fast in his life.

He kept the pace, getting to the next fire well ahead of the herd. He threw another handful of cartridges into the flames. They exploded just as quickly as the first. At the sound the stampede swerved even harder to the right. They were now rushing headlong into the pass.

The third and last fire was hardly necessary, but to keep the stragglers with the stampede, Ki threw in the last of the cartridges. He almost laughed with glee as the "firecrackers" exploded, and he watched the tail end of the herd.

"Ki! Ki!" Jessie was shouting exuberantly as she pulled her horse up alongside him. "I couldn't believe it when I saw the herd turn, I thought you were . . .

Ki was smiling. "You didn't think I'd let a bunch of dumb bovines get the best of me, now, did you?"

Jessie too was smiling. "You were a little outnumbered."

"I've faced greater dangers," he said matter-of-factly.

"I know," Jessie agreed. "That's why I was worried

about the critters. I was afraid they'd be flying right and left, dropping here and there, with you in a fighting stance right in the middle."

"I considered it," Ki said dryly.

"Of course if they were longhorns it might have been a different story."

"Undoubtedly. But we still have a stampede going," Ki reminded her.

"Oh, that's right." Jessie reached down and offered Ki her hand. "Hop on up."

Ki grabbed her hand and jumped up onto the horse's rump. "Let's see how the Chinese are faring."

"Hang on," Jessie said as she pushed the horse after the herd.

When they rode into the pass, all of Jessie's questions concerning the competency of the Double C hands were answered. The Chinese not only kept from panicking, but organized quickly to stop the stampede.

The herd had already rushed through the narrow pass and was out in the border meadow, where the Chinese were already mounted and doing a good job of milling the herd.

There are different ways of dealing with a stampede. One school of thought believes in the mill. The herd would be turned inwards, spiraling upon itself in an ever tightening radius. Personally Jessie didn't subscribe to the mill. She had seen too many cattle injured in the final phase of a mill, when a slower, clumsy animal could get gored or trampled. She found it a better practice to let the animals run, then eventually slow them to a halt.

But Jessie had no quarrel with the method. Especially now. She was just glad to see the Chinese out of danger. She glanced up the slope. There was no sign of the ambushers. She wondered about that, and it bothered her, but having no answer, she slowed her horse to a walk and watched the Chinese bring the stampede under control.

It was accomplished in an amazingly short time. That it was daytime, and there was no longer anything to spook them, probably made the herd easier to manage. But she doubted longhorns would have been as easy to control. Their horns alone would have made a mill a more delicate manuever.

The herd was now being walked slowly back along the pass they had just run through. Two riders broke away and came galloping over to Jessie and Ki.

Instinctively, Ki slid down from the back of the horse.

The first rider Jessie recognized as the foreman, Tsen-ti. The other hand she didn't know.

"Glad to see you all made it," she started with a smile. But as they drew closer her smile faded.

Tsen-ti had a broad, round face, unmarred by lines or wrinkles, and a wide, flat nose. His face had a pushed-in look to it, as if it had just been flattened by a pine board. It wasn't unpleasing; just different by Western standards. And though it was said Chinese were inscrutable, Jessie had no trouble reading the look in Tsen-ti's eyes. It was solid, tangible anger.

"What did you think you were doing?" he shouted irritably.

His attitude stunned Jessie. Caught off guard, she remained silent.

"Your fun has caused great damage," the foreman continued to rant.

"You would have fared quite worse, had we left you to the ambushers," Jessie replied coolly.

Tsen-ti seemed momentarily surprised by her answer. "Two calves are dead, and the herd has to be—"

"Do you care more about the animals or your men's lives?" Jessie snapped quickly. She did not wish to anger Gerald Scott's foreman, but she was losing her patience with the man's senseless attitude.

"It was a pointless loss. There was no need for it."

"Mister Tsen-ti, I agree. If just one of your men had been hit by a bullet it would have been a tragedy. Especially when something could have been done to save them."

The foreman's anger flared up. "We were in no danger," he exclaimed, then restrained himself quickly. Jessie caught him glancing quickly at his companion.

"That's not the way it looked from up there." Jessie pointed to the slope behind her.

"Everything was in order. We were safe, but because of your meddling two calves have died."

Jessie fought to keep her temper. A slow smile crossed her lips. "No, two calves died because you let the mill go too long. If you had stopped it sooner or let the herd run it out, you would not have lost a single animal," she answered calmly.

Tsen-ti's face turned red. Jessie never recalled a China-man turning that deep a scarlet. She hardly listened as he rattled on in his native language. But he capped off his tirade in English. "What do you know of ranching?" he spat out with contempt. "Do not tell me how to do my job."

Jessie wanted to set him straight, but she remembered that Scott had passed her off as his niece. Besides not wanting to make a liar out of him, she suddenly got the feeling that it might be wiser not to be known as a rancher and the proprietor of the Circle Star. She backed down, but only somewhat. "I would imagine that as foreman your job is looking out for the safety of your men, as well as the herd."

"You are a foolish woman!"

Ki jumped in immediately. "Let's go, Jessie. They haven't heard a word you've said."

Jessie turned to look at Ki. She was mad, and Ki knew it.

"They're safe now. We've done our job. Leave them to their chores," Ki continued. "Let's round up my horse." He didn't wait for her answer before grabbing hold of the cantle and swinging up behind her onto the horse's rump.

The second Chinese spat on the ground. "Barbarian," he said under his breath, but not so low that Ki and Jessie couldn't hear.

She waited expectantly. She had kept her anger in check; losing her temper would be an affront against her host. But she wouldn't have minded one bit if Ki gave this man the thrashing he so richly deserved.

She stared at Tsen-ti's companion. The man sat taller in the saddle and had shoulder-length black hair. In that respect alone he resembled Ki. His face was more oval in shape, with a long nose, and narrow-set eyes. Whereas the foreman's face showed easily recognizable anger, this man's eyes were cold and calculating. The eyes are a reflection of a man's soul; this man's glistened black.

It was too tempting to let Ki fight this man. But if Ki were to fight and give the man his due, it would only reaffirm the Chinese belief that the Japanese were ruthless barbarians. Ki was above that.

Moments earlier Ki had helped her overcome her anger. Now it was her turn to do the same. She reached behind her and patted Ki's thigh. "Let's go find your horse."

Ki nodded his agreement.

Jessie turned the horse and started off. She took one last look at the tall, belligerent Chinaman. "He'll get his yet," she thought to herself.

They rode in silence until they came upon Ki's horse. The roan, grazing peacefully in the shade of a cottonwood, seemed to break the spell.

"And to think you risked your life to save those ingrates. Next time we'll let 'em shoot it out all day."

"No, we won't," Ki said from behind her. "We did what we thought best, and we'd do it again."

"I don't know."

"I do. You couldn't stand by and let innocent men get hurt, Jessie, any more than you could—"

"You wouldn't think so, but that Tsen-ti and his compadre sure make it appealing."

Ki let out a laugh. "You can't let two rotten apples spoil the whole barrel."

"I'm surprised to hear you say that. No, I'm not," she

added quickly. She let out a chuckle herself. "I'm just sorry we had to save the rotten apples with the rest of the bunch. It would have done those two good to stew."

"Trouble is, the guilty ones always walk away. And the innocent men get hurt."

"Not if we can help it, Ki."

Ki laughed again. "I guess not."

Before Ki mounted up, they decided to have lunch. It was a simple but satisfying meal. It was also a little out of the ordinary. The beef jerky had a spicy Oriental tang to it, and instead of biscuits they had sticky rice balls. There were also strips of pickled turnips. At least that's what Jessie thought they were. They might be radishes or some other Chinese vegetable. She couldn't be certain; she had never had anything like them. The first bite made her mouth pucker, but by combining the rice with the sharp condiment, she grew to like the taste.

"It's different, but it gets the job done," she said as she took a last bite of rice.

"Much like the Double C cowhands," Ki remarked.

Jessie nodded. "They did seem to be doing all right with that stampede."

"More than all right, if you ask me."

"What do you mean, Ki?"

"There's something puzzling about the whole thing. But I don't know what," he said frankly.

"Maybe it just took you a bit by surprise. I felt the same," Jessie confided. "For some reason I didn't expect the Chinese to be able to ride like that. I have to admit it, though. They're as good a hand as any on the Circle Star. Of course I don't abide much with their foreman, but you can't fault a puncher for the boss he rides under."

"That's it, Jessie!"

"Tsen-ti?"

"Yes and no. Mainly it's what you said first. I guess I had reservations too about the abilities of the crew. I know I shouldn't have. . . ."

"And you of all people," Jessie chided playfully.

"I know," Ki said somewhat remorsefully. "But I had them just the same. And because of that I was willing to give the crew the benefit of the doubt. But now there's something fishy going on. . . ."

"I'm not sure I follow."

"I'm not sure I do, either. When we first came to the ridge I wondered how the Double C men came to be pinned down in that pass."

"I thought it was pretty clear."

"Is it?"

"They rode right into an ambush." Jessie said it with an unnecessary emphasis, as if she were explaining to a child. Ki, though, didn't seem to take offense.

"That's the obvious part, but then what?"

"They took to cover."

"There's where it falls apart," Ki said conclusively.

"I don't see how," Jessie said, shaking her head.

"Caught in the same situation, what would you do, Jessie?"

"I'd duck for cover too. It's simple horse sense."

"Is it?" Ki continued without waiting for her answer. "If your horse gets spooked, or if you can't ride at a full gallop, maybe. I assumed that either of those two were applicable to the Chinese. I gave them the benefit of the doubt. But the minute those cattle came through, they were right up on their horses. As you said, they can ride."

"So you think they should have ridden right past the ambush?"

"I do," Ki replied with a nod.

"And leave themselves open to get picked off, as they rode right by?"

"That brings up my other question. If there were two or three men waiting in ambush, doesn't it strike you odd that even on their first volley they didn't hit anything? Not a single rider—not even a horse?"

"Luck?"

"More luck than any cowpoke could ask for," Ki said dryly.

"I wouldn't believe it myself," Jessie agreed. "For that many men to walk into an ambush and all escape unharmed is pretty odd at that." Jessie thought a moment, then continued. "Unless the ambushers were only trying to scare off the crew. Or send a warning."

Ki didn't look convinced.

"There is a difference between rustling and murder," Jessie stated plainly.

"True," Ki agreed. "But I'm still wondering how the Double C men came to be pinned down."

"Ki!" Jessie exclaimed exasperatedly.

"Why didn't they ride hellbent-for-leather out of there?"

"We've been through this already. It made sense to get to cover."

"Jessie, they knew they were being fired upon by rifles. All they had were revolvers. Once they ducked behind those rocks, they were pinned down. . . ."

"All right," Jessie conceded. "I see your point, and yes, I would have made a run for it myself. But it's always easier to see things after the smoke clears. When someone's getting shot at they don't always make the right decision."

"They were getting shot at all right, but no one was getting hit."

Jessie laughed. "Why do I have the feeling I'm chasing my tail and getting nowhere?"

"Because we're on the trail of something, and when we catch it I guarantee it won't be your own tail sticking out of your mouth."

Jessie still had some doubts. "Ki, if you and I were trapped in there, we might have made a run for it. But if there were others, if we were with a crew, maybe I too would play it safe and run for cover. Maybe Tsen-ti was thinking of the safety of his men . . .?" She let the question drop. Jessie had dealt with the foreman enough to know that he had little concern for the safety of his men. "And stop looking at me like that," she snapped at Ki, when she saw the smug expression on his face. "You're not as smart as you think, Ki," she quipped with returning humor. "Otherwise you'd have the answers!"

"I always found it worked best if I asked the questions, and then let you solve them," Ki said with a smile.

"In other words you get to sit back and relax while I trail thieves, chase gunmen, and outwit all manner of detestable critters."

"Someone has to have the fun. Might just as well be you," Ki said with an innocent shrug.

"Great."

"Of course, if you'd rather stay at home, safe and out of harm's way . . ." Ki suggested slyly.

Jessie let out a laugh. "You win, Ki." She got up and went to her horse.

"Where to next?" Ki asked.

"Might as well head back. We won't gather any answers around here, and we have far and away enough questions."

They swung a wide loop back to the ranch house, approaching the circle of buildings from the western ridge. They were walking their horses down the slope when Jessie turned to Ki.

"I've never known you to ask a question without having a pretty good idea of the answer. It's understood there's nothing substantial to go on, but what's your theory, Ki?"

Jessie never got an answer. Below them the Double C barn suddenly burst into flames.

Chapter 5

Ki sent his horse flying down the hill. As the animal picked up speed, the ground beneath its hooves started to give way. They left a wake of loose rocks and dirt. Only its forward momentum kept the horse form stumbling. Somehow the roan's legs managed to shoot out in time to keep it from falling flat.

When they hit level ground Ki kept the horse at its breakneck pace. Flames were shooting out of the hay loft; they would need every man to fight the blaze.

The fire was well under way by the time Ki reached the corral, but the fire-fighting attempts were just beginning. Scott was furiously barking orders as the crew hastily formed a bucket line from the creek.

Ki jumped off his horse. "Where do you want me?" he asked Scott.

47

"We need every man on the line," the rancher shouted in response.

Ki took a place in line, but he quickly saw the futility of it. With most of the Double C men out on the range, the line was seriously lacking. There weren't enough men or buckets.

Scott must have been reading his mind. "Damn! It's a losing battle. Quick, Ki—up at the house there's a spade and a pickaxe. Fetch 'em from the dogtrot and meet me over there. You men keep working those buckets."

A minute later Ki brought the tools to the side of the barn.

"She's a goner, Ki," Scott said gruffly. "There ain't enough water in them damn buckets to put out a campfire. But I'll be damned if I'll let the bunkhouse and chuck house go down too."

Ki nodded. The way the wind was blowing, there was a danger that a fallen timber could set the other buildings aflame.

"We won't have time to dig a trench, but I don't think there's a need," Scott explained. "You an' me should be able to handle any sparks that fly off."

"Maybe we should get some of the other men to help?" Ki suggested.

Scott shook his head. "Too many men, and we'll be tripping over each other like a gaggle of geese. We can handle it."

"Why take the chance—" Ki began.

The rancher turned on him. Obviously Scott was not used to having his orders questioned. "On my spread, we do things my way."

It was a foolish risk to take, but Ki was not about to argue. He nodded his head.

"Even with the wind blowin' it ain't the risk it seems. I've seen other barns like it burn. They tend to collapse in on themselves. I expect this one to do the same. I should be thanking you for your help, not snapping off your head," he added with a smile.

"I understand," Ki replied.

"And besides, I'm hoping that maybe those damned buckets'll have some effect after all."

Ki turned to look at how the bucket brigade was faring when he saw Ling Ling running around. She caught his eye and came running over.

"Where's Tommy?" she asked frantically. "Have you seen Tommy?"

"He was on the line with the others," the rancher answered.

Ling Ling shook her head. "He's not there. They have not seen him." Her voice was getting desperate.

A terror seized Ki. With all the commotion he had not taken stock of the animals. He knew most of the horses were out, saddled and ridden. He turned around. The others were in the corral. The hogs and a handful of chickens were running loose out back, squealing up a storm. The barn should be empty, but he wanted to be certain. He asked Scott.

Before the rancher spoke, Ki had his answer. Scott's face turned white. "The wagon team'll be in their stalls, and Bandit, my own palomino."

Ling Ling gave a scream and started to run towards the barn. Scott reached out a hand and held her fast. "Let me go! Let me go!" she screamed as she squirmed to break free.

"You can't go in there. You can't even get near, Ling Ling." Scott's voice was heavy with regret.

"But he's in there. Tommy's in there and I have to get him." She couldn't say another word without breaking out in tears.

"He'll turn up, Ling Ling," Scott said without conviction. "And if he's in there it's too late anyway," he added softly.

All Ki could remember was Tommy's promise to take good care of the barn. With a sinking feeling he knew that if a single animal remained in the barn, Tommy would go in after it. But Scott was right; if Tommy was in there it was probably too late. . . .

Ki dropped his shovel and went running towards the barn.

"Don't be a fool, Ki!" he heard Scott shout after him. "You'll never make it out!"

Ki hesitated a minute; there was much sense in the rancher's warning. But as he turned around and saw Ling Ling standing helplessly, his mind was made up.

Had he not been so determined he might have turned back. Before he even got into the barn he could feel the intense heat against his face. He ran straight to the barn door and was about to throw it open when a thought struck him. The other side of the door could be a wall of fire. Even if it weren't, the rush of fresh air would fuel the blaze, and whatever there was that had not yet caught fire would quickly ignite.

Ki rushed to the side wall, where a stall window was open. The frame was in flames, but the central portion was just a vortex of smoke. Ki stepped back and dove through the opening.

He landed on a pile of steaming mud and manure and was thankful for it. In midair he had wondered what he would do if the stall were filled with burning hay. He realized there was little he could do.

Gratefully he rose to his feet and wiped the manure from his eyes. But a moment later he dropped back to his knees. Worse than the heat was the smoke that filled the barn. It was so thick Ki couldn't see more than a foot or two in front of him. It also made breathing almost impossible.

But along the ground there was an eight-inch zone of cooler, breathable air. Ki lowered his face almost to the mud, then on impulse scooped up a handful of the dung, and rubbed it on his face, neck, and hands. Against the scorching heat, any protective coating was welcome. If the manure could keep his skin from blistering, if it could buy him an additional moment or two before the inferno melted the skin from his bones, it was well worth it. But Ki had no delusions. At best he had only a few moments, if that.

"Tommy!" he called loudly. That there was no answer did not surprise him. He set off on his hands and knees. He tried again after a few yards, but still got no answer. He tried not to think the worst. It was possible that the boy didn't hear him. Inside the barn, the roar of the flames was combined with a loud hiss as air was sucked into the flames, then sent out in superheated currents of smoke.

Ki was working his way towards the rear of the barn. Ranch owners usually kept their personal mounts in either the first or last stall. Ki had never known a rancher to keep his horses mixed in with those of his crew. If Tommy went in to save Scott's horse there was a good chance the boy would be at the back of the barn.

Ki felt a rush of hope. Towards the back there seemed to be a small smoke-free pocket. If Tommy was still alive, that small pocket of air offered a good chance of survival. Ki hurried along.

He crawled a few more yards before stumbling into the body that lay in his path.

The boy was still breathing. Gently, Ki lifted Tommy's head. As he did so he became aware of the bump on the boy's forehead. Looking around, it wasn't hard to figure out what had happened. Off to the right an exhausted, nearly asphyxiated palomino lay on its side, its eyes wide with fright. Behind it the opened stall door was kicked to pieces.

The palomino must have been battering the stall door as Tommy approached. As the boy swung open the door the panicked animal must have reared up and struck the boy on the forehead, but before the horse could bolt it was overcome by the smoke. Toppling over had saved the animal, and for that matter the boy as well. The air just a few feet higher was deadly.

"Tommy! Tommy!" Ki shouted. The boy did not stir. Ki slapped him hard on the face. He was about to strike again when he saw Tommy's eyes open.

"Ki . . ." Though there was no fear in the boy's eyes there was an immediate recognition of their situation. "We have to get out, and Bandit too," he said with a faint smile. He started to stand.

"Don't get up," Ki warned as he held Tommy down. "We're all right for the moment."

"And Bandit?"

Ki assumed that was the palomino. "We'll get him out, too."

It wasn't only a humanitarian gesture. The animal would be useful in getting Tommy to safety. But before the horse could be of any help, Ki had to calm it. Skilled in *ninpo inubue*, an animal charming technique, Ki felt reasonably secure that in time he would win over the animal and get it back on its feet. But they didn't have time.

Keeping to his knees, Ki approached the animal. He uttered soft reassurances as he moved closer, never taking his eyes from the palomino's. Under his direct stare the horse's terror seemed to dissipate. Ki's every thought was directed towards earning the animal's trust. When Ki reached out to touch the horse's mane, the palomino rolled onto its knees.

"Good boy," Ki said soothingly. "Tommy, crawl over here, and bring that blanket next to you."

When Tommy was at his side Ki continued, "now get on Bandit's back, and lock your arms around his neck."

"Like Jessie did?" Tommy asked eagerly.

"Just like Jessie." Ki scratched Bandit's nose while Tommy got set. "Now I'm going to throw this blanket over you. It'll help you and Bandit breathe."

"Aren't you going to ride with us?"

Ki shook his head. "Someone has to open the barn door."

Just then there was a loud creaking from the rear wall. The raging fire had been hard at work rapidly consuming the timbers, and was soon going to take its toll. Ki had been aware that their pocket of air was the result of that inferno. In the swirling currents of hot smoke they had found an eddy of cooler air. He could not gauge how long it would be before the wall gave in. But from the low rumble that was coming from that direction, there wasn't much time before the wall would come crashing down.

"Take a deep breath, Tommy, and hold it as long as you can."

"You'll be okay, too, won't you, Ki?"

"I'll be right behind you," Ki promised, then threw the blanket over Tommy. Ki pulled it low to try and cover as much of the horse's face as possible. It didn't cover much but at least it shielded the animal's eyes.

Holding on tight to its mane, Ki led the palomino to the door. On the way they passed the lifeless bodies of the horses—the wagon team. Another long, torturous groan emanated from the back wall. They were getting out just in time.

"Damn!" Scott exclaimed. "Where are they? The whole barn's going to go any second."

Ling Ling said nothing, but continued to stare at the burning inferno.

Just then Jessie rode up. "Tommy's not anywhere I can find him."

A minute behind Ki, Jessie had ridden into the yard. When she saw Ki race to the house, she followed on horseback. On her way she ran into Ling Ling. The housekeeper implored her to help find Tommy. Jessie reeled her horse around and took off for a fast lap of the grounds and neighboring hills.

From their faces she could tell her pronouncement was not news. She followed their anxious looks. "Oh, no," she said involuntarily. Then it hit her. "Where's Ki?" she asked nervously. Scott turned to her, but didn't respond immediately. That was enough of an answer.

Jessie took off for the barn.

Scott, quick on his feet, lit out after her. "There's nothing you can do, Jessie. It's suicide to go in there."

That stopped her, or at least changed her direction, for after a brief hesitation she ran towards the bucket brigade.

She grabbed a bucket of water from the hands of a startled Chinese, and after removing her Stetson, poured the water over her head. She ran up the line to the next bucket and did the same, this time keeping her hat on.

Earlier, a herd of stampeding cattle had physically kept her from helping Ki, and she was forced to stand by helpless. But she'd be damned if she'd let a burning building stop her from coming to his aid. It wasn't bravery that prompted her, but self-preservation. Jessie couldn't live with herself knowing that she let Ki burn to death while she did nothing but watch. Her thoughts weren't even that well defined. Her concern for Ki came as second nature. She was just glad that she had the foresight to douse herself with the water. Otherwise, Scott would be right. It would be nothing but suicide.

Inside the barn, Ki held his breath as they rushed through the smoke. His lungs, trained by deep meditative breathing, were not under any undue strain. His eyes, however, were another story. There was no exercise, no mental trick that could keep the acrid smoke from burning his eyes. Tears streaming down his cheeks only clouded his vision more.

He anticipated as much as saw the location of the door. There were no flames shooting out from the door, but smoke was streaming off the wood. Ki knew better than to touch the smoldering beams. He stepped back and kicked at the door.

Ki then went to slap the horse on the rump, but it was unnecessary. At the smell of fresh air, Bandit bolted towards safety.

The door swung open wider. Ki heard a large crash. Then he was knocked off his feet. He felt something hard and burning strike between his shoulderblades as he was pitched forward. A breeze of cool air rushed against his face, then everything went black.

In the moment before he came to, Ki was seized by an involuntary panic. He had to raise his head; he had to have air. He lunged forward, but then realization struck. He was lying in the horse trough, with his head submerged under water, when consciousness began to return.

He opened his eyes and saw anxious faces peering down at him.

"He's okay!" Tommy was the first to shout.

"You're a lucky man, Ki" Scott began. "When Bandit came flying out of that barn the whole shooting match went up like a tinder box."

"The back wall caved in?" Ki's remark was half statement, half question.

"That it did. And a rafter fell square on your back."

Ki gave a small chuckle.

"What's so damned funny about being nearly burned to death?" Scott wanted to know.

"I had a feeling about that door," Ki answered. "I went in through the window, but didn't count on trouble on the way out."

"Well, you almost bit off more trouble than you could chew."

"Live and learn," Ki remarked philosophically.

This time it was Scott's turn to laugh. "I'm standing here chewing the cud with a man thats got himself a face full of hard-baked horseshit. Lets get on up to the house and get you cleaned up."

Just then Ki noticed that Jessie was also dripping water. "You look like you had your moment in the trough too," he said with a smile.

"You two must be of like minds. She was just about to go in after you. Good thing you made it to the door," Scott informed him. "She probably would have dragged you free herself if Ling Ling didn't get to you first."

Ki turned to the housekeeper. He wanted to say something, but couldn't find the right words. "Thank you," he said simply as he started to pull himself up. But the movement caused him to wince in pain.

Under his stare, Ling Ling blushed and turned away, but not before she saw him flinch.

She spoke out in Chinese. Instantly, four of the crew reached for him and lifted him out of the trough.

"Gently," Ling Ling admonished, as the men carried him up to the house.

They placed Ki on his bed and, after removing his wet clothes, covered him with a sheet. A moment later Ling Ling came in carrying an empty bucket and a bowl of steaming water. She sat down on the edge of the bed.

"First we'll clean you up." She pulled a bowie knife from her apron pocket and started to scrape at Ki's face.

"Hard as adobe," Ki quipped lightly.

"Don't move," Ling Ling scolded. But her tone was not harsh. "I don't want to cut you."

"I wouldn't mind," Ki muttered inanely.

"Shh."

While Ki was being cleaned up, he heard Scott yelling in the other room. The rancher was calling Tommy down on the carpet. Ki couldn't hear all the words clearly, but Scott was really letting into the boy for not only risking his own life but for endangering Ki's as well. The lecture was not uncalled for; Ki understood the point Scott was trying to make. What surprised him, though, was when the one-way conversation took a turn.

"And damn it, boy, didn't I tell you to move those barrels of pitch?" Scott was screaming. "When I tell you something I expect it to be done. Not tomorrow, not later today, but now! If you had moved those barrels like I told you to, the damned barn might never have gone up so quickly."

"Yes, sir," the boy responded weakly.

"Is that all you have to say? Two horses dead and a man injured and all you say is 'Yes, sir.'?"

"I'm awful sorry, Mr. Scott. You gotta believe me. I moved those barrels just like you said."

"Then how come I don't see them around? Don't lie to me, boy, or I'll take a switch to your hide."

"Yes, sir."

"Now git!"

Ki was watching Ling Ling's face. With every harsh word shouted, her eyes glistened with compassion.

"He's a good boy. He did a brave thing going in after those horses."

"You did a braver thing, Ki."

I'd walk through a hundred burning buildings to hear you speak like that, Ling Ling, he thought to himself.

Suddenly he became aware of the burning in his eyes. He blinked them shut.

"I'll get something for that," Ling Ling said. She left the room and returned a minute later with two slices of cucumber. "Keep these on your eyes."

The cool vegetable did indeed soothe Ki's tired and irritated eyes, but he regretted not being able to watch Ling Ling as she continued to wash his body.

There was a gentle tap on the door. "Yes," Ling Ling called out.

The door opened and Tommy entered. "I just wanted to thank you, Ki, for what you did."

57

Ling Ling stood up. "I'll return in a few minutes to dress your back." With that she left the man and boy alone.

"And I'm awfully sorry," Tommy continued.

Ki wasn't, but he didn't say that. He took the cucumber slices off his eyes. "What Scott said was true, Tommy. You shouldn't risk your life like that. An animal is not worth dying over." The boy did look ashamed. "But I also want you to know what you did was a brave thing."

Momentarily the boy beamed proudly, but then he shook his head. "It was a dumb thing."

Ki laughed. "Sometimes the only difference between the two is the outcome. But don't repeat that," he added with a smile.

"I won't," Tommy said, returning his smile.

"Oh, and Tommy, where were those pitch barrels?"

"I moved them, honest I did."

"I believe you, Tommy. . . ."

"I wouldn't lie to you, honest, Ki. . . ."

"Where were they before you moved them?"

"Just to the left of the door."

"Not against the back wall?" Ki wanted to be absolutely certain.

Tommy shook his head. "They were right next to the old buckboard."

"One other question I've been meaning to ask. The door was shut. How did you get into the barn?"

"The old root cellar, around the side."

Ki smiled. "Smart thinking. One other thing, Tommy. Could you get Jessie for me?"

"Right away." Tommy left quickly, eager to do anything for Ki.

Ki placed the cucumbers back on his eyes. He was startled by Jessie's voice.

"I must say that's an improvement over the manure."

"It feels a lot better, too," he said, leaving the cucumber in place. "Jessie, any reason why a barn door would be closed in the middle of a work day?" he said getting right down to business.

"Bad weather," Jessie answered, not catching on.

"On a day like today."

"That is odd," Jessie said thoughtfully, as she grasped what Ki was getting at. "The door was closed."

"And the fire started along the back wall," Ki remarked.

"Meaning?"

"Just thought it might come in handy to know."

"You're getting at something, Ki, and I wish you'd just spit it out."

"Ki laughed. "Jessie, if I knew I would. And you'd be the first to know."

"So these are just some more of your famous unanswered questions."

From under his vegetable mask he smiled. "Don't feel obliged to get me an answer right away. I just wanted you to know what I was thinking."

"How can anyone figure what a man who wears first manure, then cucumbers, would ever be thinking," she said with a laugh. But her laugh died quickly as the door opened.

Ki removed his eye patches just in time to catch Ling Ling and Jessie staring awkwardly at each other.

"I was just leaving." Jessie explained self-consciously, then did just that.

★

Chapter 6

Ki lay on his side and stared at the wall. Physical pain was not keeping him awake—after the aloe salve Ling Ling had applied, his blistered back felt much better—but the ointment did nothing for his psyche.

He clung to every word the woman had spoken, studied every gesture and expression she had made. He was like a starved man feasting on her beauty, a thirsty man drinking in her being. But whatever he was, he was not being himself. He could barely talk in her presence, and whatever he did manage to say seemed either silly or unimportant. He yearned to express what he felt. But how could he share anything with her when he couldn't understand it himself?

Like almost everything else he had encountered on the Double C there was more here than met the eye. Ling Ling represented much more than just the beautiful woman she was. But for all his staring at the wall, Ki couldn't figure out what.

He was still getting nowhere when he heard the door creak open. The sound of soft footsteps made his heart stop.

"Ki?" came the whispered question.

He rolled over to face the door.

"I was hoping I wouldn't be waking you," Ling Ling said softly. She placed the short, fat candle on the floor by the bed.

In the candle's soft glow, Ling Ling was even more beautiful, more desirable. There was something very enticing about the way her long, dark hair fell against her white nightgown. Ki felt a moan well up from deep in his soul, but he had no idea he actually emitted a sound until Ling Ling looked at him with concern.

"Does your back pain you much?"

Ki shook his head. "No."

"I brought some oil. It will help." She sat down at the edge of the bed, rolled back the sheet, and gently pushed him onto his stomach.

The oil, or the administration of it, did indeed soothe, at least at first. Ling Ling's small hands worked the oil gently into his skin. She started between his shoulderblades, and slowly worked her hands in ever widening circles. For a moment Ki thought if he experienced nothing more than this in his life he would be content.

"It is called snake oil, but it is not made from snakes," she informed him matter-of-factly.

The difference between her soft, loving hands and her indifferent words left Ki acutely aware of his longing.

"You are very strong, Ki," Ling Ling remarked as her hands kneaded his hard muscles. "But very tense," she continued. "You must learn to relax."

The strangest feeling coursed through Ki; he felt like crying. Without thinking he rolled over to face her. He was unaware that he had a throbbing erection.

Ling Ling couldn't avoid the large pole that stuck straight out. She didn't try to. She took hold of Ki's shaft, and slid her oily fingers gently up and down.

The feel of her hand, and the realization of his throbbing hardon, caused Ki to gasp. At his utterance, Ling Ling squeezed harder. The exquisite pleasure of her touch quickly dispelled the mortification that Ki was also feeling.

"Is this what you want, Ki? I owe you that much for saving Tommy."

Anger seizing hold of him, Ki slapped her hand away. "I don't want you to repay me. I want you to give me something." He knew what he meant, but he didn't know if what he said made any sense.

Ling Ling, though, seemed to understand. "I can't give you anything, Ki. I have nothing to give."

"That's not true. You have something very precious, very dear, to give."

"No," she said shaking her head. "I cannot. You love another—Jessie."

"No."

"Then you love someone else."

"I have loved many," he said simply.

"Oh, have you?" Ling Ling said coolly.

It was ironic, Ki thought to himself, that their first meaningful conversation was working out so poorly. "I don't know," Ki said changing his mind. "I'm always travelling, always just passing through. I have met many women; maybe I have loved some."

Ling Ling let out a gentle laugh, but it seemed to Ki there was as much scorn as humor in it. "Your life does not seem that lacking. . . ."

"I have a duty. An obligation to the Starbucks. First to her father, and now Jessie."

"Your sense of devotion goes deep."

Ki became aware that by oversimplification he was doing Jessie an injustice. "It is not only devotion," he explained. "Much has passed between Jessie and I. I owe her my life, and I have saved her from death many times. That forms a strong bond."

"You are a valued vassal," she said with contempt. Ki's explanation did nothing to help the situation.

"Ling Ling, please, listen. My life is my duty, I can't change that, nor would I choose to, but what I feel in my soul, what I feel for you is—"

Ling Ling stood up, silencing him. She picked up the candle and walked to the door. Her last words were spat at him. "Good night, samurai." The door shut silently behind her.

Ki was left in the dark with his own confused thoughts. The chasm between him and Ling Ling had grown even wider. On top of everything else, their racial differences now loomed as another barrier.

Samurai, samurai. The word held so much hate, and filled him with a deep remorse. Where had he heard that word, where had he felt such a stinging rebuke? He turned to the wall, but his vision fogged. His eyes filled with tears.

San Francisco seemed a long time ago. But it hadn't been really that long. Ki had forced himself to forget. But now it all came back to him. . . .

The door creaked open. There was no flickering candle, no light to see, but Ki knew who it was. He could smell the faint aroma of snake oil, and the warm scent of the woman.

Ling Ling sat down on the bed. "I can't deny my desires, Ki, any more than you can walk away from your obligations."

"Ling Ling, I understand now what you were saying," Ki began excitedly.

"It was just jealousy. But that doesn't matter now."

"No, Ling Ling. You made me understand something. . . ."

"And you made me understand something." She leaned over and pressed her mouth against his. It was a deep kiss, full of passion.

Ki did not want to break away, but he wanted to share his thoughts before he lost his resolve to do so. "I want you to know that—"

"And I want you," was all Ling Ling said before resting her lips lightly against Ki's.

When her tongue darted out, Ki lost his resolve to say a word. He grabbed her and pulled her close to him. He needed no stimulation, but the feel of her soft breasts through her gown had his pulse rushing. His hand reached to cup her round breast and her nipple sprang out to meet his palm.

His rod was again throbbing hard, and again Ling Ling took immediate notice.

"It is like the rest of you. Very hard and very beautiful," she said as she stroked it. "But this time I will not let you push me away."

Ki had no intentions of doing that, but he didn't feel it was necessary to bother saying that. Even if he had wanted to speak, all he could have uttered was a soft moan.

Ling Ling began to stroke Ki with both hands, her fingers gliding expertly over the sensitive skin. Whether by design or just to get comfortable, she pivoted around and swung her legs up towards the head of the bed. Ki slid her gown up to her waist and ran his hand along her smooth thigh.

His hand went over the roundness of her hips and down the curve of her waist. He grabbed her and pulled her to him. Without further preliminaries he buried his face into her soft mound. Her curls were long and smooth, her flesh moist and warm. He drank her in, like a thirsty man. . . .

Ling Ling stretched out her tongue and flicked at the round head. It was tentative, and all the more exciting for it.

Ki let out a loud moan. But not a sound was heard. His cry of delight, though muffled deep between Ling Ling's thighs, did not go unnoticed.

The vibrations from Ki's mouth sent a tremor through Ling Ling's body. Her tongue caressed Ki's length. Ki's hips bucked off the bed. His organ slid into her mouth. She held him firm between her cheeks, exerting the most wonderful suction.

Ki buried his tongue deeper, sucking at her nectar. It was now Ling Ling's turn to moan. But again no sound was heard, as her mouth was stuffed with Ki's organ.

Ki felt his tremor start somewhere deep inside of him. Ling Ling must have felt it too. Her hand squeezed his shaft, and he exploded deep in her throat.

Ki locked his arms around her waist, and flicked his tongue lightly across the folds of her flower. Ling Ling began to quiver uncontrollably, her body squirming over him. Only Ki's muscular grip kept him at his task. Suddenly her body went totally rigid. Then an endless time later it went limp, and sagged against him.

They lay arm in arm, satisfied and at peace. But the feel of Ling Ling's breath against his neck and the gentle heaving of her breasts soon had Ki stirring again.

Ling Ling nibbled at his ear. "I thought you were asleep."

"I thought you were asleep."

"Dreaming, but not asleep." Her hands traced patterns across his chest, slowly moving down across his flat, muscular stomach. Eventually her hand brushed against the pole that was stretching ever upward. "Oh," she said with surprise and delight.

This time it was she who dispensed with the preliminaries. She rolled on to her back and spread her legs wide. "Take me, Ki."

Ki leaned over and took her budding nipple into his mouth.

She sighed and uttered a weak complaint. "Don't make me wait."

Ki lifted his head a scant inch. His tongue continued to tease her. "We have all night. . . ."

"Once you're on top of me, yes. But I need to feel you now," she pleaded.

Ki understood. He rolled on top of her, sliding in easily.

"Yes, deep." Ling Ling groaned loudly.

"It was too urgent before. Now I want it to be slow and loving."

"Yes, Ki. Yes. Any way you want it." She lifted her knees to her chest.

Ki had the sensation of being engulfed by her. Though his words spoke one way his body had a mind of its own. He lunged into her. His hips pistoned full force against her.

Underneath him, she rocked back and forth, meeting each thrust with a movement of her own.

Together they increased their speed. Ki took hold of her shoulders, taking long deep strokes.

The bedsprings started to squeak. "We should be quiet," Ling Ling gasped between heavy breaths. "We'll wake the whole house."

"No one can hear," he assured her, but he slowed his movements all the same.

Ling Ling gave a disappointed sigh. "I guess maybe only Jessie could hear."

"Do you care?" Ki asked slyly.

"We should be quiet," she repeated. But her body started to rock faster and faster. Soon the bed was squeaking once more. "She is a heavy sleeper, though, isn't she?"

Ki didn't answer; he couldn't. He started to buck faster than before.

Ling Ling wrapped her calves around Ki's neck. He lowered himself on top of her, plunging in deeper than before. Their lips met, their bodies melded together, and they moved in unison.

They didn't know how long it went on. They were lost

in each other's bodies. But then a long-awaited and very overdue spasm wracked Ling Ling's body. At her first tremor Ki erupted. In a blaze it was over.

Holding each other they slept till morning.

The next day, Ki stayed in his room. It was understood that he needed his rest, that fighting the blaze had drained his energy. With a wry smile he wondered how much his condition was due to the inferno that was released last night—the heat of the passion that had passed between him and Ling Ling.

The more he tried to think of Ling Ling the more visions of San Francisco haunted him. It was a long time ago, he tried to tell himself. That fact, though, offered little comfort. It was ironic that Ki had tried so hard to remember, and now he wanted nothing but to forget.

But how could he forget Su Ling? And the pain... After her tragic death at the hands of the Tong, Ki had lost every reason for being. His heart, his very desire for life, was wrenched from him. Having been disgraced by the Tong, she sought revenge and salvation. There was only one form available, only a single narrow path, and she took it willingly. She had died bravely, sacrificing herself for the sake of her family, for the family honor. Honor. It seemed such a senseless word in the face of one so young and beautiful. But Su Ling could do nothing else. And that was why Ki loved her so.

Su Ling! Ki replayed those final moments. He saw every action, every move, as he had a hundred, a thousand times before. And still he could not be certain. Could he have saved Su Ling? Could he have prevented her death? It was a question he couldn't stop asking. He laughed drolly to himself. *Yes, Jessie, I am a master of questions that have no answer. My life is a question that has no answer.*

How could he forget Su Ling? He thought of the first time he had laid eyes on her. She was selling food from the family cart, down at the wharf. The way her eyes lowered as she gave herself to him, knowing the risk, the censure for loving a barbarian. A slow smile spread across his face. Next to one such as she, how could he be anything but a barbarian? How could he forget her?

A sudden understanding hit. He was clinging desperately to her memory. Ki was well versed in meditative skills; had he really wanted to he could have quieted his mind, blanked out the sorrow, at least momentarily. But he did not. He kept his mind focused on the past, on what was gone, on what could never be again.

He had loved Su Ling. Totally, with all his being. And he had lost everything. As long as her memory stayed alive he would never venture that much again. He would never lose, never be hurt like that again. It was clear to him now. The devotion, the duty, the Starbuck empire were all excuses. As long as he had those, and Su Ling's memory, he need not fear.

But Ling Ling, with her gentle eyes and heart-stopping smile, threatened all that. He sensed that instantly, the moment he first laid eyes on her. But was he captivated by her because she reminded him of Su Ling? Was he trying to bring back the past? Or was that same spark that attracted him to the woman in San Francisco now drawing him to the housekeeper? Was he as helpless as a moth drawn to the flame, or was he following his destiny?

Only time would tell. For all Ki knew, Ling Ling could be the reincarnation of Su Ling's spirit. For a brief moment the two women merged together in his mind. He couldn't differentiate the softness of one and the beauty of another. After Su Ling he never thought he would meet another like her, never meet anyone that could touch his being like she had. But he was proved wrong. It was more than he deserved. He should be thankful.

But Su Ling hung there like a specter. How could he forget her? And did he ever want to? More questions. And no answers.

• • •

That night Ling Ling came to him again. He wanted to tell her about Su Ling. In fact he started to, but Ling Ling quieted him, turning the night from one of talk to one of action.

Their improved technique was matched only by their heightened desire and increasing affection for each other. As they lay together, sweat glistening on their bodies, Ki knew a deep bond was forming.

This time he would not be silenced. He had to tell her. He had planned to explain in only the briefest terms, but as he talked, the words poured forth. She listened impassively, politely, not saying a word. But when Ki finished she made love to him again, slowly, passionately, till dawn.

Chapter 7

It was late morning when Ki dressed and wandered down to watch the work on the barn. Little was done the day before; the wood was still smoldering. But today, the crew had already razed what was left of the building, and was busy carting away the charred wood.

Ki moved next to Jessie. "I always had a feeling for stone barns," he said as he sniffed the charcoal smell that hung in the air.

"They don't burn as well, that's for sure," Jessie answered.

"My point exactly."

"And they don't have to be rebuilt as often."

"As a matter of fact I've never known a stone structure to ever need rebuilding. But then I haven't seen one that was over five hundred years old," he added with a smile.

"Ki, the oldest barns I've seen aren't even half that!"

"Jessie . . ." Ki said patronizingly.

"Even back east around Boston, the barns don't predate the fifteen hundreds."

"Jessie . . ." Ki repeated.

"Uh-uh, Ki, I'm not going to let you get away with these broad generalizations and exaggerations you pull, no matter how impressive they may sound."

Ki let out a laugh.

"And the old Spanish missions, whatever their age, are mostly 'dobe," she continued. "So I don't see how you can give me that line about five-hundred-year-old stone barns."

"I didn't say barns."

"Whatever. It won't wash," Jessie said, very self-satisfied. "I got you this time."

"Castles, Jessie."

"What?"

"Edo Castle, a magnificent stone structure built in 1457."

"Ki!"

"Actually that's when it was finished. I don't know the exact date they started construction, but it must have taken years."

"Ki, I don't see the relevence Japanese castles have to Western barns."

"I'm simply pointing out the soundness and durability of stone construction," he answered genially. "And then there's Hamachi Castle, which predates Edo by another hundred years, but I never personally laid eyes on it."

"Well I'm glad you're feeling better today," Jessie said curtly.

"Thank you."

"I heard you moaning in your sleep last night!"

Ki quickly changed the subject. "Maybe I'll try and impress Scott with the efficacy of a stone barn," he said as he started to walk off.

"It's not up to him anymore."

Ki turned. "What do you mean?"

"I've bought the place," she informed him. "Least I agreed to."

"Then do I have to start all over again, about long lasting stone?" he said absently as he thought about Jessie's decision.

"Don't bother, Ki. There's too much good timber around. That's one of the reasons I decided to buy the Double C. The need for lumber will grow, and as we thin some of the hills, we'll create more grazing land."

"Sounds like a wise decision," Ki said, unreasonably hurt that Jessie had made a decision without discussing it with him first. Though he knew there was no reason to; he never took an active role in running the Starbuck business, and Jessie knew that. But she usually talked matters over with him before she acted.

Jessie must have read his mind. "After the fire, Scott had just about had it with his run of bad luck. He was fed up, ready to cash in his chips. And I had already seen enough to make up my mind. There was no sense in putting it off. Why make him fret needlessly?"

"That was kind of you, Jessie," Ki said sincerely. "Another person might have stretched it out, waiting for Scott to lower his price."

"It was a fair price as it was, Ki. I wouldn't want to take advantage of him."

Ki nodded. "It's not the Starbuck way to chisel on a deal."

"Anyway," Jessie continued, "Scott was going to town today to arrange for a shipment of lumber. Since he was already making the trip, I told him to have his lawyers draw up the papers. There was no point having him go twice."

"I understand."

"I was going to come talk to you this morning, before he left, but from the sound of it you were having a rough

72

night. I figured I'd let you have your sleep," Jessie explained further.

"I do understand, Jessie. I was just being childish."

Jessie smiled. "You're allowed your moments, Ki. Once every ten years," she added under her breath.

"About as often as I intend to run into a burning wood barn," he said with a smile.

"Ten years from now I'll remember that."

For a moment Ki's mind wandered. Ten years from now where would he be? With Jessie still? And what of Ling Ling?

"But then I don't plan to let anybody burn down my barn."

Jessie's comment brought Ki back to the present. "You think someone torched the barn?"

"Don't you?"

"I'm pretty sure of it."

"I also had a talk with Tommy," Jessie said slyly.

"Then you realize that you're not only buying Double C timber and land, you're buying Double C problems."

"I realize that, Ki," Jessie said firmly.

"Rustling, arson, an unruly foreman, and who knows what else," Ki said offhandedly.

"I intend to find out."

"We could have investigated before you made the purchase," Ki started.

"We could have," Jessie agreed.

"But . . . ?" Ki asked. Jessie shrugged, and Ki finished his sentence. "But since he is a friend of your father's you wanted to spare Scott from the ensuing problems."

"Something like that, I reckon."

"A commendable sense of allegiance. I really mean that, Jessie," he said proudly.

"Scott built this ranch, came here when it was nothing, and made his mark. That's enough for any one man. Let him retire in peace. We'll carry on the fight for him. We're better suited for it."

"I wouldn't underestimate him, Jessie."

"He's a tough old coot, I'll grant you that. He's earned a rest."

"There might be more here than we realize," Ki cautioned.

"And that's one of the reasons I'm buying the spread. I want a free hand cleaning up the Double C. And I don't want anyone getting in our way."

There was a determination in her eye that reminded Ki of her father. "Alex would be proud," he said softly.

"I hope so."

Ki spent the rest of the day looking for clues. He didn't know what exactly he was looking for, and that made the job even harder. By midday he admitted he was getting nowhere and headed back to the house.

As he passed the cookhouse, Tsen-ti stepped out. It was not a coincidence. The foreman was coming directly towards him.

Involuntarily, Ki stiffened. He did not want an unpleasant exchange to mar the day. Therefore it was all the more shocking when Tsen-ti stopped a few feet from him and lowered his head in a respectful bow.

"You are a brave man, Nipponese." he said, then turned and walked away.

It was a simple gesture, but Ki did not underestimate its meaning. Perhaps he was wrong about the foreman. But he was never to know.

After dinner, Ki stepped outside to join Jessie on the porch. He would rather have spent the time helping Ling Ling with the dishes, but there was something he had to discuss with Jessie. He had thought about it all day, but kept putting it off. He was not one to procrastinate, and the fact that he was doing so bothered him.

He pulled up a chair next to Jessie and sat down. "It's no secret that we're not finding any answers."

"It may take some time," Jessie said calmly.

"Perhaps, but if you're not looking in the right places, all the time in the world won't help."

"True. What do you suggest?"

"There are some things I'd like to know about the crew. But I'm not going to find out anything around here."

"No loose lips, huh?"

"I wouldn't know, I haven't even gotten that close," Ki said with a chuckle.

"Have you tried?" Jessie asked. "No, that's not fair," she added quickly. "I know you try your best. Some things are just not possible."

"That's why I was thinking of going to town. Maybe a few days there will reveal something."

"Well, like you said, we're getting nowhere here."

"What the folks in town have to say about the Double C might open up a lead. I also would like to learn a thing or two about the Lazy M."

"The outfit that fella Lawry works for?" Jessie asked. Ki nodded. "Well, I reckon it's a start," she agreed. "Meanwhile I'll hold down the fort till Scott returns."

"And when will that be?"

"He should be back tomorrow."

"Good. I wouldn't want to run into him in town," Ki explained.

Jessie understood. Once in town, Ki was not about to announce his business. An accidental meeting with Scott might ruin Ki's cover and foil his scheme. "You might run into him on the road, but I suppose that won't matter."

"It shouldn't."

Jessie stood up. "Then if I don't see you in the morning, good luck. I'm going to have a hot soak and turn in."

"Good night, Jessie."

A few minutes later Ling Ling brought a pot of hot tea out to the porch and sat on the floor, her head resting in Ki's lap.

"Ling Ling, tomorrow I'll be going away for a couple of days," Ki began.

75

"I know," she said softly. "I heard." Ki looked surprised. "The kitchen is not all that far away," she said with a smile, "and voices carry."

"Then you understand?" Ki asked hopefully.

"It is your duty." This time there was no mockery in her voice.

"I would rather stay here with you and do nothing but watch you all day and hold you all night."

"You would get underfoot, Ki. And I have work to do."

Her tease proved to Ki that she really did understand. She was a jewel, but he didn't tell her that. It would have sounded too corny.

"If I don't go, I wouldn't be fulfilling my obligation to Jessie. I would only be pretending."

"How dishonorable." She was smiling as she said it, but she was not poking fun.

"I will come back as quickly as possible," Ki promised.

"I know. Now—shall we wait for the moon to rise or shall we go to bed?"

"Whatever you'd like."

They decided to sit outside a while longer. The air was cool, and with the barn downwind, the sweet smell of damp grass replaced the odor of burned wood. Ki stroked Ling Ling's hair and listened to the sounds of the evening. At the creek the bullfrogs were calling out to one another, while from all sides the crickets chirped noisily. The musical hoot of an owl drifted in on the breeze.

Eventually Ki told Ling Ling about his brief encounter with Tsen-ti.

"It was his way of thanking you for saving Tommy."

"It seemed unlike him to even bother," Ki remarked.

"He is a proud man, but well-meaning. What you did meant a great deal to him."

Ki looked confused, "But after our first meeting—"

"You did not know Tommy and Tsen-ti are cousins," Ling Ling said quickly.

"No, I had no idea. And you are the boy's aunt?"

Ling Ling nodded and smiled. She then proceeded to explain the relationships. "It's really quite simple," she said as she finished.

"I'm sure it is, once you know everyone," he admitted. There was no denying the confusion that was written all over his face.

"I'll go through it once more, but pay attention," she said playfully. "Tommy's father, Zen Mo, is my oldest brother. Tommy's my nephew, I'm his aunt."

"That part is easy," Ki said with a smile.

"Tsen-ti and Zen Mo are cousins, Tommy and Tsen-ti are cousins. Simple, isn't it?"

"Put that way, yes. But I'd swear that wasn't the first version I heard."

Ling Ling giggled. "I left out some of the matriarchal entanglements, and a few of the unnecessary brothers, and used everybody's shortened common names."

"It also helped not going back three generations," Ki added.

Ling Ling gave an innocent shrug.

"I don't know why I never thought of asking before, but how is it that the crew is all Chinese, or even part Chinese for that matter?"

"It is a long story."

"We have all night," Ki said gently.

Ling Ling smiled. "There are better things to do with the night, Ki."

He was not about to argue. "Is there a short version?" he wondered aloud.

Ling Ling nodded. "You will miss a lot of the good parts, but I can try."

"I'll miss more if the tale takes all night," Ki said devilishly.

There was no argument from Ling Ling. She started right in. "Briefly. Zen Mo saved Mr. Scott's life."

Ki shook his head. "Too brief."

"Zen Mo was working on the Central Pacific. Mr. Scott was a construction foreman."

"I didn't know that," Ki said.

"An accident occurred. Zen Mo risked his own life to save Mr. Scott. They became close friends. When they parted, Scott made my brother promise that if he was ever in need he would come to him for help. Well, when the railroad was finished my brother was not one to become a houseboy or servant. He learned to ride and rope. He became quite good at it, too. There were other Chinese that also learned. One day, Zen Mo and his cowpunching coolies showed up here, and Mr. Scott hired them all."

"One day I'd like to hear more of the details," Ki said with interest.

"There were a few points I glanced over quickly," she admitted.

A thought struck Ki. "The whole crew can't be ex-coolies; they're too young."

"The original crew was, but these are friends and relatives. In the Chinese community Zen Mo was quite a legend. Others, though not many, would make a pilgrimage to learn how to lead the life of an American cowpoke."

"And Scott hired them all?"

"Just about. He said someone had to pay the national debt you Americans owed the Chinese for building your railroads."

"He's a good man," Ki said with a nod.

"And besides, they were good hands," she added defensively. There was just a touch of righteous indignation that made her eyes sparkle. Ki's heart melted.

He took hold of her hand and stood up. "Let's go inside. . . ."

Ki woke with a start. He wasn't sure what it was he heard, but he was pretty certain it came from next door—Jessie's room. Immediately alert, he jumped into his pants. Ling

Ling stirred. "Stay here," he ordered, then went running out of the room.

Not knowing what to expect, he threw open Jessie's door and crouched down in a fighting stance. But there was no call for action. Jessie was sitting on the edge of the bed facing the window. Her chambray night shirt barely covered her long, shapely thighs.

She turned and smiled at Ki. "Some unknown suitor has an odd calling card," she said as she held up a round rock.

Ki was not amused. He never was when danger threatened Jessie.

Jessie read his mind. It was not difficult to do; she had seen that expression many times before. Ki's eyes narrowed, his jaw set with a grim determination. "Ki, it's nothing to worry about. I'm all right."

Ki took the rock from Jessie, feeling its weight in his palm. "Had this hit you in the head . . ."

"But it didn't."

He went to the window, and peered through the broken shards of glass. His hand still played with the rock as his anger grew.

"Insults are one thing. Physical violence is another," he said angrily as he turned to the door.

"Ki, it's too dark to look for sign," she said hastily.

"I'm not going out there looking for tracks," he said firmly.

"Ki, wait."

"I'm going down to the bunkhouse."

"Ki, what do you expect to do, roust them all from their beds and check all their eyes for Mister Sandman?"

"I'll know who did it."

"How?" she started to ask. Then she quickly asked the more important question: "And then what?"

Ki didn't answer.

"You can't take on the whole crew," she said nervously, though she knew in his angered condition, he could very well try. Looking at his resolute face, she changed her tactic. "Only one man threw the rock. The others are probably innocent, good workers."

"I'm not so sure about that anymore, Jessie."

"What happened to your philosophy of not letting a bad apple spoil the whole barrel?"

Ki thought a moment then shrugged. "That was theory. This," he said, holding up the rock, "is reality. There is a difference."

Jessie sensed there was more fueling Ki's anger than just the rock. "Ki, I've been shot at before and you've never gotten this mad. It was only a rock."

"There's more principle in this rock than in those bullets."

"Principle! A lump on the head doesn't send someone to the grave."

"Jessie, the crew has been insolent since we arrived. If we don't put a stop to it now, the Chinese will never show any respect."

"I agree, Ki. But this is not the way to do it."

"I can't think of a better way. Besides, your safety is entrusted to me. They know that. This is a flagrant insult, a slap in my face."

Just when Jessie thought it was useless to try and reason with him she hit upon what she hoped would be the magic word. "Ki, you can't go in there and kick their Chinese asses. You're not a barbarian."

The rock suddenly became heavy in his hand. He remembered the shame Su Ling was made to feel by her family for loving a 'barbarian.' His arm lowered. "No, I guess I'm not."

Jessie saw his mood change and pressed her advantage. "What we have here is a simple labor relations problem. I'll talk to the crew first thing in the morning."

Ki nodded. He had seen Jessie address groups of workers before, men who were scared or angry and sometimes both. She had taken a mob, on the point of violence, and calmed them. She had a way of expressing herself that seemed to win people over. "I'm sure that's best," he agreed.

"And Ki . . ." She retraced her steps back to an earlier question. "How would you know who threw the rock?" That he would know she didn't doubt; she just wanted to know his method.

"I'd check the boots for dew."

"And if he didn't wear any?"

"I'd check their feet."

"I can see you tickling all their toes," she said with a giggle.

"Is everything all right?" asked a sweet voice.

Ki turned. Ling Ling stood in the doorway. A candle flickered and softly illuminated both their faces.

Only moments ago, Ki's anger had been on the verge of boiling over. Now with Ling Ling standing beside him, it evaporated into thin air.

Jessie smiled. "Everything is fine now."

Chapter 8

In the morning, Jessie had Ling Ling assemble the crew outside the main house. Jessie stood on the top stair and waited patiently for the men to quiet down. It only took a moment. Apparently they were curious to hear what she had to say.

First, she bowed politely. There was an awkward pause, but then the men returned the gesture. "I know you all have work to do," she began, "so I'll make it fast. As I'm sure many of you know, I'm not Gerald Scott's niece. My name is Jessica Starbuck. Ranching is my business. I own a spread in Texas, and now I own the Double C."

A buzz went through the men. Jessie continued. "At least I will once Mister Scott returns with the deed. That may not come as a total surprise. At least one of you men knew. He voiced his opinion last night."

Jessie paused and studied their faces. So did Ki. But there was no indication who the guilty party was, or if the crew had any knowledge of the incident.

"I can understand a certain amount of worry on your part. So we'll put the halter to it right now. No one collects his time unless he wants to. You're all welcome to stay on. Every one of you. But I warn you: I expect an honest day's work from each and every one of you. If you can't do that, or you can't abide taking orders from me or Ki, then roll your blanket now and hit the trail."

Ki continued to watch the crew. His eyes came to rest on the tall Chinese, the one who had accompanied Tsen-ti in the argument after the stampede. The man was talking quickly. He was way beyond earshot, but the look in his eyes told Ki he was giving instructions.

"And one other thing," Jessie concluded from the porch. "Gerald Scott put a lot of trust in you all. I hope you won't prove him wrong." She turned and went back into the house. The men broke up and went back to their work.

Ki hurried to Ling Ling. "Who is that tall one?" he asked directly.

Ling Ling turned to watch the men depart. Ki couldn't believe she didn't know which man Ki was referring to. There was only one tall Chinese in the crew, but he pointed him out anyway. "There, that one."

"That, that is Chan Pei."

Was it Ki's imagination, or did her voice falter. Sudden jealousy flared up in him. "Who is he?" he demanded.

Ling Ling shrugged. "A hired hand."

"There's nothing more you want to tell me?" Ki persisted.

Ling Ling shook her head and looked away.

Ki regained control of his emotions. She was an attractive woman. It was foolish for Ki to think she had been leading a celibate existence. There was no reason for Ling Ling to confess to her past romances. Ki accepted that. If she said nothing, it was because there was nothing more to say. Ki let it drop. "I understand, Ling Ling," he said softly. "It was wrong of me."

In fact, Ki had never been more wrong.

The day turned balmy as Ki headed down the trail for To-panga Falls. Ki was expecting the sun to break through the haze, but as the day wore on, it seemed unlikely the cloud cover would burn off. Rain would have been equally welcome, but Ki suspected the cooling shower wouldn't come till late afternoon. It was going to be a hot, muggy trip.

A few miles from the ranch house, Ki pointed his roan to the ridge that ran parallel to the road. At the higher elevation there seemed to be a faint breeze blowing through the tops of the trees; it would offer some relief from the warm, sticky air that clung to the back of Ki's neck. But that was only a secondary benefit. Ki wanted to get off the road and get a better look at the surrounding land.

The slope wasn't heavily forested and the roan steadily made its way through the scrub oaks and pines. They soon gained access to the ridge top. Ki swiveled in the saddle to take in the three-hundred-and-sixty-degree panorama. Though Ki wasn't on the highest peak, he still had a good look at the lay of the land.

Behind him, tucked between distant hills, was the Double C ranch house. He couldn't see any of the buildings, but the thin trail of smoke that emanated from the cook-house gave away its location. Surrounding the ranch, and spreading out in a wide strip, were the heavily forested hills Jessie and Ki had ridden through a few days earlier.

Ahead of Ki the land became rougher. The hills were more jagged, jutting up from the earth in steep angles. Rocky shale sides replaced timbered slopes. The valleys still had sufficient grazing, but clearly the Double C had carved out the best chunk of land.

Below and to the right, Ki could see the road. It stretched out for quite a way, slowly veering to the left, then falling out of sight as it turned in sharply. Ki decided to stay in the hills and cut across to where the road vanished. But it was hardly a shortcut. As the crow flies it was a more direct route, but having to travel up and down the many gullies made for much slower going. If Ki were pressed for time the road would have been a better choice. But from the road he could never spot strayed or stolen cattle.

Ki gave the roan its head and let the animal pick his way down the slope. Underfoot the gravel was loose, and it was wisest to let the horse find its own footing. Off the slope, Ki followed the gully, then climbed the next ridge. There was no pattern, no system, no method to their trail. There didn't have to be. Only by chance would Ki find what he was looking for. And after a few miles of this, Ki realized his chances were slim.

There were too many gullies and ravines in which to hide rustled stock. But Ki's sidetrack was not without purpose. It added another curiosity to his already long list of unanswered questions. If Ki were stealing cattle from the Double C, he'd bring them up here. The chances of them being found were, as Ki was learning firsthand, almost impossible. Yet they had found signs of cattle being rustled in the southern pastures, in meadows that would easily allow the stock to be tracked. Of course the cattle could have strayed; there was no firm indication that there was rustling going on. But Ki didn't need positive proof. There were enough questions, enough suspicions in his mind, that he knew without a doubt something strange was going on.

At a stream Ki dismounted and let the horse water. He unpacked the saddlebag and decided to have lunch. As he pulled out the muslin sack, his hand found something hard and metallic. A slow smile crossed his face as his fingers wrapped around the grip of a Walker Colt. Ling Ling must have slipped the revolver in when she packed his lunch. She had not wanted Ki to travel unarmed. She didn't realize that although he carried no firearms he was hardly without a weapon. There had been no call for Ki to exhibit his martial arts. Ling Ling would have no knowledge of his skill and capability. She only knew that Ki was travelling alone, and it was wise for a man on the trail to have some sort of protection in case of emergency. He was not offended by the gift. Ki knew the gun did not imply that he could not take care of himself. It was just Ling Ling's way of saying "be careful."

Ki ate his meal and thought longingly of Ling Ling. He was incredulous that he already missed her; it had been only a few hours. With childlike simplicity, he reasoned the sooner he got to town the sooner he would return to the Double C and Ling Ling.

He remounted and was headed back towards the road when suspicion began tugging at him. He had assumed that Ling Ling's action—packing the gun—stemmed from innocent concern. But maybe there was more to it than that. Maybe the gun was not only a reminder to be careful, but a hidden warning.

Someone had thrown a rock at Jessie; it was quite feasible that they would try worse with him. If the warning had not scared Jessie, perhaps physical violence might. It took a certain kind of lowlife to beat up a woman, but most of the Chinese hands would have no hesitation in roughing up her Japanese companion.

That he had saved Tommy, that he had earned Tsen-ti's brief admiration, would not help him out here. The Walker would. Was that why the gun was in his saddlebag? Did Ling Ling suspect, or know, Ki was in danger?

He kneed the horse into a gallop, making good time in the flat ravine. When he saw the road up ahead he slowed his horse to a walk. As the pace slowed, so did his thinking. He took a firm hold on his imagination, and brought his suspicions under control.

First there was no proof of rustling. Second, the rock-throwing incident could have been an isolated event. Jessie's talk to the men might very well have ended the crew's unrest. And as far as the Walker in his saddlebag, it might be nothing. . . .

Ki was just about convinced when he heard the rifle shot.

He burst into the road just as a wagon thundered past. He could see the driver lying in the wagon bed as the team raced out of control. The man was Gerald Scott.

Ki lit out after the wagon. He knew he would catch it, but could he catch it in time? Scott was perilously close to the tail end of the wagon. If the man was still alive, the fall from the wagon could be the stroke that killed him. A bullet lodged near a vital organ could be jarred loose, an injured artery could be torn open, or his neck could simply break on impact. Ki couldn't be certain Scott was even alive, but it seemed the rancher was consciously trying to flatten himself against the wagon bed. Ki urged his horse to go faster.

As he came abreast with the wagon, he saw Scott's face, white and drawn in pain. The man was alive. It would have been easier and wiser to stay in the saddle and pull alongside the team, eventually slowing them to a walk. But Scott was only seconds from falling out of the wagon. Stopping the wagon would be unimportant if the rancher lay dead in the road.

Ki pulled his roan as close to the speeding wagon as he could. He slipped his left foot from the stirrup, and, leaning over, tried to grab the wagon's sideboard. But the horse kept shying away, well aware of the danger of galloping too close to the runaway wagon. Ki steered the animal in closer, then made a desperate dive from the saddle. He kicked hard with his right foot, making sure that his foot wouldn't get hung up in the stirrup and that his momentum would carry him into the wagon bed.

He landed on his right shoulder, his legs flipping over him. It was an ungainly somersault, but looks and grace hardly mattered now. He got to his knees almost instantly, then turned to grab hold of Scott. At that moment the wheel went over a bump and the wagon bucked high into the air. The rancher started to slide off the back. But Ki already had a firm hold on his collar. His other hand went quickly to the man's arm, and as gently as he could, Ki pulled him back into the wagon bed.

Ki noticed that his hand was covered with blood. The wagon had to be stopped, and Scott's wounds needed attention. Ki climbed over into the seat. But the reins were not there. They were dragging on the ground behind the team. Ki stood up and lowered his body into a horse-stance. The classic martial arts fighting posture—widespread legs, bent knees, straight back—was equally good for stability, and was perfect for just such a situation. Had Ki wanted to, he could have remained steady and firm, unaffected by any jolt or lurch of the wagon. He had done it before, even atop speeding railroad cars. But his intention was not to remain planted on the spot.

He was preparing himself to spring onto the back of the closest horse, where he could lean over and grab the panicked animal by the bit. But the timing had to be perfect. A slight misjudgment and Ki would wind up in the dirt. Possibly the wagon wheels would miss him, but Ki did not want to take that chance. Besides, Ki would be no help to Scott if he were lying face down on the ground. He had to make his first and only leap right onto the back of the animal.

He lifted one leg onto the top of the front faceplate. He couldn't balance himself long like that; he would have to jump momentarily. He took a quick look at the road ahead, making sure there were no turns, then studied the horse briefly to get the animal's stride. He flexed his thighs and got ready to spring. Then his eyes caught a sudden movement.

He dropped to his knees, his chest hanging half out of the wagon, his hand snaking out. It was one smooth movement that took no more than a second. But when he straightened up, the reins were held tightly in his hand.

Going over a rock, the leather straps had snapped up in the air. Ki had caught the movement, and then the reins. He pulled back on the leather and slowed the wayward team. *Like snatching a trout with your bare hands,* he thought to himself with a smile.

After bringing the wagon to a stop, he hopped into the back to have a look at Scott. The rancher, with great effort, was pulling himself up to a sitting position.

"Take it easy," Ki said as he helped the man.

"Damn beasts," Scott said between clenched teeth. "A nag that ain't trained to gunfire'll make damn good tallow. I'll see to that."

Ki smiled. Anyone who could curse and be that angry wasn't seriously wounded. "More than likely, those animals just saved your life."

"I won't be showing no gratitude," Scott said gruffly. "Damn near broke my neck."

"But whoever was waiting for you only got one shot."

"One shot was enough to spook the team and pitch me onto my back."

"A convincing act," Ki remarked.

"What in tarnations are you talkin' 'bout?"

"Whoever took that shot at you must have thought you were dead. I don't see anyone coming down the road."

"That low-down, snake-in-the-grass bushwhacker ain't half the shot he prides himself to be."

Ki laughed. "Lucky for you."

"But I reckon I did put on a good show, toppling over like that." Scott shook his head. "Another six inches higher and he'd have splattered my brains."

Ki nodded. "Now let's have a look at that shoulder."

Surprisingly, Scott didn't argue. He let Ki rip away his shirt. The bullet had gone in at the top of the arm, right below the shoulder. But Ki's hand had blood on it after he pulled the rancher back into the wagon. He eased Scott forward and took a look at the shoulderblade. His back was coated with blood. It only took a moment to find the hole behind the man's armpit. "The bullet's gone clear through." He manipulated Scott's arm, and the rancher winced in pain. "Hurt much?" Ki asked.

Scott shook his head. "Nothing too fierce," he said bravely.

"I can't be certain but I don't think it even chipped a bone. A doctor can tell for sure. But for now let's get this bandaged."

Ki was about to rip his shirt when Scott stopped him. "My shirt's already ruined," he said with a weak smile.

"All right," Ki said with a nod. He ripped a few strips from the man's shirt and soon had Scott's shoulder tightly bandaged. "I think that should stop most of the bleeding. It should hold till we get you to a doctor."

"I don't need no damn doctor!" Scott exclaimed.

"We'll head to town, and see what the doctor says," Ki said firmly.

"Doc Nayer?! He's an old drunk. Ain't even fit for horses."

"I want to make certain that wound heals clean," Ki answered. He said nothing about wanting to make sure the bleeding stopped.

"Ling Ling's been nursin' the Double C for years. She got salves and ointments that do the job just fine, Ki. If you're worried about that wound, she'll take better care of it than any sawbones I ever knew."

Ki hesitated a moment. He knew enough about herbal remedies and Oriental medicine to know of their effectiveness, and he had to admit the salve Ling Ling applied to his blistered back had helped.

"And besides, we're as close to the Double C as we are to Topanga Falls," Scott reasoned. The rancher pulled himself to his feet. "I'm much obliged for your help, Ki, but now I think I'll head on my way. An' I was headin' back to my spread," he added stubbornly.

Ki knew when he was licked. And it did make as much sense, if not more, to head back to the ranch. "All right, you win," he said with a smile. "Lie back and relax."

"No need. I'll sit up front with you," Scott said. Ki gave a disapproving look and started to speak, when the rancher cut him off. "Not only will it feel better if I sit up and don't put pressure against my shoulder, but I got a hankerin' to get a look at that dirty skunk if'n he tries something like that again."

"I don't think he will. He no doubt thinks you're already knocking at the pearly gates. If he didn't he would have shown up by now," Ki answered. "But if you'll feel more comfortable sitting up front, let's get going." With Ki's help Scott climbed into the seat, and the wagon started down the road.

"Have any idea who might be taking a shot at you?" Ki asked Scott.

"Damn straight I got an idea," the rancher snapped. "Got more'n an idea. I wasn't born yesterday, Ki, an' if that bastard thinks he c'n get away with usin' Gerald Scott for target practice he's got another thing—"

"Who?" Ki interrupted the tirade.

"Who? Who else but that Mercer!"

"Mercer—the man you think has been rustling your stock?"

Scott nodded. "First my critters, now my land."

"Even if he has been stealing from you why would he now try and murder you?" Ki wondered aloud.

"'Cause he knows I'm about to sell, that's why." The rancher patted his shirt pocket with his good hand. "When I get Jessie's signature on this deed, it becomes official."

"So you think Mercer was trying to stop that by bushwhacking you?"

"Maybe not Mercer himself; the man's too yellow to do his own dirty work. But one of his plug-uglies for sure."

"But if you didn't sell to Jessie you'd have sold to someone else. What would he gain by—"

"A dead man don't sell nothing," Scott interrupted sharply. "The Double C would rightfully go to my brother

91

back east, but more'n likely Mercer'll pull some shenanigans and have the place put up for public auction."

"But with a proper will, there shouldn't be a problem."

Scott laughed. "Boston's a long way off, Ki. The legal arm don't nearly extend that far."

Ki understood. Executors and city councils were not all that diligent in following proper procedure. Ki had seen many a spread fall into the wrong hands through some fancy legal footwork.

"Even if that happened, what makes you think Mercer would wind up with the Double C?" Ki wondered aloud.

"A man like Mercer doesn't reach for his iron, 'less he knows the gun's loaded."

Ki understood the reference, but it didn't really answer his question "That still doesn't explain—"

"Mercer's damn chummy with Sheriff Harmon and that fancy-pants dude that passes for a district judge."

"Is the sheriff crooked?"

"It wouldn't surprise me one bit," Scott answered flatly.

"But as far as you know he hasn't—"

The rancher shook his head. "But any friend of Mercer's not to be trusted."

"Why is that?"

"Mercer's a known rustler. Got his start that way," Scott explained distastefuly. "Just to be associated with the likes of him proves you ain't got much respect for the law."

Ki didn't pursue it. Scott's obvious rancor for his neighboring rancher made further discussion pointless. And the course of conversation changed quickly when they came upon Ki's roan grazing by a hackberry.

"Now don't get me wrong, Ki. I ain't one to look a gift horse in the mouth, but just what were you doing way out here?"

Briefly, Ki explained his purpose. He was careful, though, not to mention his desire to feel out other people's opinion of the Double C and its Chinese crew.

"Well, Ki, I suggest you get back on your horse and turn right around."

"I was thinking of that," Ki agreed. "But I didn't want to leave you alone."

"Ah, hell, Ki. You can see I'm doing fine. Besides, you might even be able to pick up the tracks of that stinkin' bushwhacker."

Ki didn't need to be persuaded. This ambush could be the first clue in finding the answers to Ki's questions. If Ki could follow this thread it might lead him back to the spool. Or more importantly, the person holding it.

The rancher stared at Ki. "Quit stewing it over," he said plainly. "You got better things to do than nursemaid an injured rancher. Get on your way," Scott added with a smile.

Ki nodded, climbed down from the wagon, and called to the roan. The next minute he was kicking up dust as he headed back towards Topanga Falls.

★

Chapter 9

It wasn't hard for Ki to find the place that hid the ambusher. First he located the spot where Scott was shot; the gouge marks left by the bolting wagon team were his clue. Then, judging from the rancher's wound, Ki estimated the angle at which the bullet must have entered. He straightened his arm along the line of the trajectory, and sighted down the end of his finger. Moving a few degrees in each direction he soon spotted an outcrop of rocks halfway up the nearest slope.

He left his horse alongside the road and climbed the grade on foot. As he went, he looked for hoofprints, but he wasn't surprised when he didn't find any. More than likely the ambusher would have tethered his horse in the distance and gone in on foot, just as Ki was now doing.

Once behind the rock, Ki studied the ground. There

were a few boot marks, but no one print was sharp enough to determine the man's size or weight. He was examining the dirt when he caught sight of a shiny metal cartridge lying in the moss. He picked up the cylinder and, after a brief inspection, dropped it into his vest pocket. There was no real need to save the shell; he'd immediately identified it and the gun it must have come from.

There was no mistaking the .44 cartridge. They were the most popular bullet in use. Any number of handguns, from the converted Remington army model to the widely used Colt Peacemaker used that caliber cartridge. But a revolver wasn't used this time. It was unlikely that the ambusher would have bothered to break open the gun to remove only one bullet when there where still five live rounds chambered in the cylinder. Even if some personal obsession had compelled him to do so, the cartridge would have dropped right out of the gun. Ki would have found it behind the rock. This shell was a few feet away. The spent cartridge had been ejected from a rifle as the ambusher prepared to take another shot, then deemed it unnecessary. As far as Ki knew, there was only one rifle that would take a .44 cartridge and eject it that many feet away—the Winchester .44-40.

The carbine, also known as the Winchester '73, was not an uncommon gun. The fact that it could take revolver shells made it a very popular choice, and in the years since its introduction its use had become widespread. Though it was likely that many men owned one, it was another clue, another piece to the puzzle.

Ki returned to his horse and rode around to the back side of the slope. After a few minutes' search, the half-eaten leaves of a boxwood told him where the bushwhacker's horse had been tethered. He found sign leading both in and out of the ravine, but they retraced the same path. Ki followed the trail, but about a mile later it came to a shallow, rapidly flowing stream. He knew better than to waste his time cutting for further sign. The trail was dead, and it wasn't by accident.

Though Ki would have preferred to trace the would-be assassin, even this dead end told him something. The man knew the lay of the land, and knew that after the murder there might be an investigation. He was leaving no trail behind. The man was careful and smart. That was another piece to the picture.

Topanga Falls surprised Ki. It was not the dusty cattle town he had expected. Topanga Falls was the railroad depot for the whole valley, and as such had grown as more and more of the land became settled. There was a long main street, old and established, and a secondary one that sprang up parallel to the first as the town expanded. Smaller streets branched off from the two, and were dotted with the houses of the townfolk.

If saloons were any indication of prosperity, business was thriving. This town had three, all accomodating different tastes and styles. The Gold Nugget, the largest and wealthiest of them all, was the dancing hall and gambling room. Even without going in, Ki knew the saloon would be lushly appointed with silver mirrors, red velvet drapes, polished wood tables and deep, padded chairs. As Ki rode past he could see the large stage and the many gaming tables.

Across from the stables was the Sagebrush, another large saloon but of simpler tastes. It was the type of place a trail crew could gather and let off steam. A broken chair and table would hardly be missed.

The last establishment, in the center of town, had a sign that read simply HAMMEL AND KORN. It was much smaller, and as its position indicated, was the oldest of the three saloons. It looked to be the place that catered most to a regular clientele. It was the type of place where the bartender would pour your drink and the cook would rustle you up your favorite meal. Instinctively, he liked that saloon the most, but it wouldn't best serve his purpose.

He turned and headed for the Sagebrush. There, a passing drifter wouldn't attract any attention. He had a quick beer, then asked directions to the Lazy M, Tom Mercer's ranch. Although he couldn't follow the trail of the ambusher there was a chance he could pick it up in the vicinity of the Mercer spread, if of course the would-be assassin was a Lazy M hand.

Before leaving town, Ki stopped off at the general store to pick up a sack of biscuits and jerked beef. As an afterthought he added a blanket to his purchase. Up in the hills, a slight breeze could turn the warmest night bone cold.

Ki spent that night tucked in peacefully under the stars. It was a clear, warm night, and the smell of pine and wet grass pleasantly filled the air. He had found no incriminating tracks leading into the Lazy M. There were plenty of tracks, but none of them matched the prints he saw in the ravine. Of course, a shrewd man could have had a change of horses waiting for him somewhere downstream.

There was no proof either way, so Ki decided to keep an eye on the ranch till the next day. By then word would have gotten around that Scott had been shot and that he had survived. If Mercer had anything to do with the ambush, that news might cause some activity on the Lazy M.

Ki kept up his vigilance throughout the night, but more often than not his thoughts strayed to Ling Ling. He was alternately warmed by thoughts of her—her bright eyes; her sensuous smile; the feel of her soft, smooth skin—and frustrated by his desire to be with her, instead of out hiding in the hills. He yearned to feel her warm body nestled up against his. Instead there was the dry feel of pine needles.

He was thankful when at sunrise he saw signs of life stirring down in the ranch. A small trail of smoke snaked skyward from one of the two small cabins. A bit later, two men stepped out, went to the shed, saddled up, and rode out. Ki wasn't certain, but the two riders looked like

Lawry and Jake, the men Scott, Jessie, and Ki ran into their first day in the valley—the men Scott accused of rustling.

Ki decided to follow them. If they were up to no good, he would catch them red-handed. There wasn't much timber; the land was much more rugged than the Double C end of the valley. By keeping to the high slope and staying far enough behind, Ki avoided detection. The two riders never looked back. There was no reason to. If they had, Ki would have become instantly suspicious; honest men tend not to look over their shoulders.

Two hours later all of Ki's suspicions vanished when the two Lazy M riders stopped at a windmill. They dismounted and one of them grabbed a bucket from his saddle. Ki had seen enough. He should have noticed the bucket of grease from the start. If he wasn't so intent upon finding Lawry's hand in the cookie jar, he would have had a clearer head. Maintaining windmills was a typical summer job on any ranch. Proper upkeep meant the head and shaft had to be greased regularly. With a soft curse for his stupidity he turned and headed back to town.

His anger with himself lasted till he got back to Topanga Falls. It was a minor error, Ki knew, but it was symptomatic of a larger, more costly mistake. He had let his desires come in the way of rational thinking. He had let his yearning for Ling Ling cloud his thinking. He was looking for the easy solution, not the right answer. He wanted to find the Lazy M riders guilty, guilty of anything, just so he could return to Ling Ling. It had cost him nothing this time, but he might not always be so fortunate.

But there was no point in fretting any longer. Ki put his horse in livery and asked the stable boy the best place for a good meal. He got his answer, nodded his thanks, then walked over to Hammel and Korn's.

This late in the afternoon the saloon was almost empty. The single customer sat against the near wall nursing a cup of coffee and slice of pie. The man had his hat low over his eyes, and Ki took no notice of him. He walked up to the bar. "Is it too late for a hot meal?" he asked politely.

The bartender, a stout man with thinning gray hair, a round face, and a long handlebar mustache, looked up and studied Ki briefly. "You're too late for midday an' too early for supper," he said plainly. "But I won't have a hungry man turned away." He wasn't quite smiling, but his voice was full of good nature.

"Thanks," Ki said sincerely. "I've heard good things about your cooking, and after last night's meal of biscuits and jerky, and no breakfast to speak of, I could use a good meal."

The bartender looked him over gravely, and Ki had to break into a laugh. "I'm not panhandling," he said with a smile, once he realized his mistake. For a moment, Ki had come on too much like a drifter, down on his luck and penniless. "I have the money to pay," he added quickly.

The bartender shook his head. "Wouldn't be the first meal I've given away, though I shouldn't be announcing that. Have a seat." He gestured to a table. "Steak an' potatoes and gravy?"

"That'll be fine," Ki answered as he took a table against the far wall.

A moment later the bartender returned with a plate of hot biscuits. Ki started in on those, and before he knew it his meal had arrived. It was everything he hoped it would be, and then some. Ki wiped his mouth and leaned back contentedly. "'Bout the only thing I could use now is a day or two of work," he said to the bartender as the man picked up the empty plate.

"Can't help you there, friend. I already got me a swampy."

"I'm not averse to sweeping out a saloon," Ki said with a smile. "But I'm a better ranch hand. Any good outfits that might be hiring?"

"Can't say," the bartender replied as he walked off into the kitchen. But Ki sensed more than saw him steal a look at the gentleman at the other table.

Ki continued his questioning when the bartender returned with a pot of coffee and a slice of blueberry pie. "What about the Double C?"

"The Double C?" The bartender seemed surprised to hear him mention it.

"I hear tell it's a pretty big spread," Ki explained quickly.

The other patron lifted his head. "It won't do you any good, 'less of course you're Chinese," he said in a resonant voice. He studied Ki closely. "Your eyes don't look right for a Chinaman," he observed correctly. "Half-Chinese?" he wondered aloud.

Ki looked across the room. The man sat tall in the chair, with an ease that said he was not often challenged. His Stetson was pushed back to reveal a head of long, sandy hair and a face that was bronze and tough, yet unlined with wrinkles. The man was undeniably handsome. His eyes were a shade darker than his complexion, and though they showed no malice, their gaze held fast on Ki.

Ki decided to take no offense. "Half-Japanese," he replied flatly.

"Too bad," the man began, until he saw Ki's reaction. "I mean as far as getting work. They have an all-coolie crew."

"Maybe not anymore," the bartender interjected. "Scott just sold his spread."

"Where'd you hear that?" the bronze fellow demanded.

"From the horse's mouth. Gerald was in here chowing down last night."

"Why didn't you tell me?"

The bartender shrugged. "Just didn't get around to it, Tom."

"Who'd he sell to?"

"Some big Texas outfit."

"Well, he won't be missed."

The bartender looked displeased. "I wish you two could have settled your differences. He's not a bad sort."

The tall man placed some money on the table and stood up. "His own men steal him blind, and the fool does nothing but call me a rustler. He's lucky he unloaded the spread while it was still worth something," he added as he headed towards the door.

"What about the Lazy M?" Ki called out quickly. The man, opinionated as he was, could be a valuable source of information, and Ki did not want to let him leave just yet.

The man turned to face Ki. "What about it?" he said with a smile.

"Just wondering if they needed another hand."

"The Lazy M? You don't want a job there, friend."

"Why's that?" Ki wondered aloud. "Ain't the work honest?" he said fishing.

"It ain't the work, it's old man Mercer. He's mean. I hear tell he once shot a hand he saw loafing on the job." He brought his index finger up to the middle of his forehead. "One shot. Right here."

"That so?" Ki remarked calmly. "Not many can get away with cold-blooded murder."

The tall man nodded and looked at Ki sternly. "That man Mercer makes his own laws. No one crosses him and lives to tell of it."

"Seems like a man like that would constantly be needing new hands."

The tall man shook his head. "He's had the same men working for him for years."

"Why do they stick around?" Ki asked.

The man moved closer to Ki, and lowered his voice. "Rumor has it he keeps them chained up at night. But the simple truth is, no one knows more about ranchin' than Tom Mercer. You stick with him and in a few years you know more about raisin' calves than a mother cow."

"I know enough about cattle," Ki answered lightheartedly. "I need to learn more about money in my pocket."

The man shrugged. "You might do best trying some of the homesteaders at the northern end of the valley. Don't expect them to pay much, though."

"Thanks. I might just do that."

"Either way, if you're heading out towards Tacoma, you'll pass the Lazy M. Mean as he is, Mercer's always good for a hot meal and a place to lay yer head." With a wink to the bartender, the tall man stepped outside.

"Friendly sort," Ki remarked to the bartender. "One of the homesteaders?"

The bartender's eyes twinkled. "Him? He's a rancher."

"Small spread?"

"The Lazy M." The bartender let out a hearty laugh. "That's Tom Mercer."

Ki quickly paid for his meal and rushed outside. He didn't have to go far to catch up to Mercer. The man stood at the edge of the boardwalk. Surrounding him in a semicircle that bowed out into the street were a half-dozen Double C men. At the moment nothing was being said, but from the look on their faces it was not a social visit they were paying Tom Mercer.

For the first time Ki noticed that Mercer was not packing a gun.

★

Chapter 10

"So Scott sent you out on one more errand," Mercer said evenly. "He couldn't leave the valley till he took care of me, could he?" He kept a careful watch on the men that stood around him, but slowly eased over to the horse that was tethered to the rail just a few feet to his left.

Ki didn't think the rancher would make it. He moved forward. "Does Scott know you're here?" he asked loudly.

The Chinese just then noticed him. "This is no business of yours," one of them answered.

"I think it is. Does Scott know you're doing this?" Ki repeated.

"Scott don't know nothing," another answered.

Ki's face paled at the implication. Although the wound didn't seem lethal, Ki was not a doctor. It could have taken an ugly turn.

The Double C man read his thoughts. "He's all right. "Now, out of the way."

Mercer took a quick look at Ki. "There's no sense in you taking a beating too, friend."

"I don't see the sense in anyone taking a beating," Ki replied.

Mercer chuckled at that. "Some things ain't left to reason. A man don't always have a choice."

Ki was still determined to try and avoid a fight if possible. "Does Tsen-ti know you're here?"

There was no answer, but the question seemed to put a bit of hesitation into some of the men, until one of them, a shorter man with a flat bull head, yelled back at Ki. "Be careful, barbarian, or you might get hurt yourself," he said with a grin that exposed smoke-stained teeth.

The comment only served to harden Ki's determination. If it came to a fight, this thick-headed one would be the first to have his teeth knocked out. Ki was pulled from his thoughts by Mercer's voice.

"See what I mean? They ain't capable of reason. The only way to knock some sense into them is to butt their yellow heads together."

"You've bushwhacked your last man, Mercer," one of the Chinese yelled.

"Well now, old man Scott must really be feeding you the bull these days. I've gone from rustlin' and cheatin' to bushwhackin'. I'm one bad hombre."

Ki couldn't be certain—the man did have a flair for facetiousness—but it seemed that Mercer really had no idea of what the Double C crew was talking about. Ki was going to bring that to the attention of the Chinese vigilantes, but he didn't think it would do any good. He also didn't want to blow his cover as a passing drifter. He had already made one or two slips that revealed he was not just an ignorant stranger, but Mercer didn't seem to catch them. It was best to keep his mouth shut.

"Your bad days are over, too," Bull-head yelled again.

For a brief moment Ki thought the confrontation would be nothing more than verbal. He felt just the slightest pang of regret; Bull-head was asking to be taught a lesson. But considering the odds it was probably best if violence was avoided.

Ki had just finished that thought when he caught sight of Chan Pei standing off in the distance. Bull-head kept turning to the tall Chinese as if waiting for orders. When Ki saw Chan Pei nod his head, he knew the period of verbal abuse was over. Ki moved closer to Mercer and readied himself for the attack that he knew would be unleashed any moment.

Forewarned though he was, Ki was still surprised when the assault hit. Like Mercer, he had been watching carefully for the first move—the first punch, the first kick. But there was no single strike. When the fight began, all six Chinese rushed in together.

Ki reacted quickly. His left leg shot out and caught the first man in the chest, sending him staggering backwards. Ki landed lightly and swung his other leg around in a low *mawashi-kubi-geri*. The sweep kick caught the second Chinese behind the ankle, and the man toppled forward. But the third man coming in on the far side managed to grab onto Ki's leg. He clung to Ki's thigh like a drowning man to a log. There was no damaging power behind the hold, but it encumbered Ki and restricted his movements long enough for the other two to pounce on him.

Ki brought his knee up hard into the clinging man's face. The blow, though, had little effect. Ki couldn't get enough leverage or force into it. He was about to try it again when the second man scrambled to his feet and grabbed hold of Ki's other leg. As he started to lose balance, he caught sight of Mercer. The man's earlier comment gave Ki an idea. With each hand he took hold of a Chinese head. He had a good lock of hair in each hand when he brought his hands together. The two heads butted together loudly and Ki felt the stranglehold on his legs relax. But he had already lost his balance and was falling over backwards. It didn't matter. He hit the ground and rolled free. When he hopped to his feet, the two Chinese lay slumped in the dirt.

Meanwhile, though Mercer was not faring as well, he was still holding his own. But at that moment, another rush of the Chinese got the best of him. The third man came up on Mercer's blind side, and all four went crashing down in a pile of limbs, with Mercer on the bottom. The very nature of the pile-up ensured that Mercer would not get seriously hurt. There was little exposed target, and there was no room to throw an effective punch. But Ki wanted to get the Chinese off the rancher as quickly as possible.

He grabbed the collar of the top man, pulled him aside, and hit him with a powerful roundhouse punch. Disappointedly, he realized it was not Bull-head. He had reached and grabbed hold of the next Double C man when he felt a heavy weight slam into his back. He was knocked onto the pile of struggling bodies, where he remained momentarily pinned.

From his position, he saw Chan Pei advance towards them. He saw something glint in the man's hand: a blade, out and at the ready.

Ki reached behind him but couldn't get a hold on the man that lay on top of him. He tried again, but with no better results. Chan Pei was moving closer—Chan Pei, with the deadly silver spike. Ki reached behind him again, this time making his own hand hold. He dug his powerful fingers into the neck of the topmost Chinese, and closed his grip. He felt his fingers break through the skin, but he continued the viselike pressure until he was sure he had a firm grip, then he peeled the man off of him like bark off a tree.

Ki quickly lifted himself to a crouch, then brought the hardened edge of his hand to bear on the neck of the next Chinese. The swift *tegatana-uchi* rendered the man limp, and Ki cast him aside. That worked so well he did it again with the next man on the pile. But this time there was no need to push him away. Mercer took care of that for him with a strong lift of his leg. The rancher then rolled free of the last Chinese. Apparently that last man had been no problem at all. He had been the closest to the rancher, and during the whole pile-up Mercer had pelted the man's face continuously with his fist. They were short strokes, but the hardness of Mercer's knuckles eventually took their toll.

Smugly, Ki admitted to himself that he had been wrong. It was possible, even in that tight mass, to get injured. The unconscious Chinese with the bloodied and puffy face was ample proof. And though it was hard to make out the likeness, there was no mistaking the bull-shaped head of the man that lay face up in the dirt.

Now that his adversaries were not pinned down and helpless, Chan Pei backed off. Ki thought the fight was over, but then two more men charged at them. They were the same two who had rushed at Ki earlier. They were now just coming to their senses. Ki leaped high into the air and let go a flying snap-kick. The *mae-tobi-geri* exploded in one man's face, and the Chinese dropped like a lead weight.

Mercer meanwhile was dispensing with the second Chinese. He waited till the man was almost upon him, then he sidestepped quickly and took hold of the stumbling Chinaman's collar. With a mighty heave he swung him around and sent him flying through the air. The man's trip ended abruptly when he crashed head first through the plate glass window of Hammel and Korn's Saloon. Ki suspected that Mercer had seriously bloodied another face, but the thick curtains that fell down around the man's head kept Ki from being certain.

If that in itself did not end the fight, the emergence of the bartender, toting a sawed-off shotgun, did. "You men get on yer horses, and get back to the Double C, before I have the sheriff lock you all up," he ordered loudly.

"Sorry 'bout that window, Hammel. I'll be sure to take

care of it for you—" Mercer started to say.

"No need," the bartender replied. "T'wasn't yer head that broke the glass." Again his face was somber, but his voice gave in to the humor. "I'll see to it that those that are responsible will make good."

Mercer picked up his hat and brushed it off against his leg. "Much obliged, Hammel," he said with a smile. He then turned to Ki. "Reckon I owe you too, friend. And seein' as how you can't stay here, get your horse an' come along with me. I think the Lazy M just hired a new hand."

Ki nodded his thanks. "I'll meet you at the stables."

Mercer climbed up onto his mount. His hand reached down and pulled a Winchester from its boot. For a moment Ki had his doubts. Was it possible that Mercer really did shoot Scott? Ki quickly reminded himself that this was not the only Winchester in town. He didn't know much of the rancher, but he seriously doubted that Mercer was the type to wait in ambush for a defenseless man. If Mercer had a score to settle he would do it out front and in the open.

From his hip Mercer pointed the rifle at the Chinese. "If any of you have the idea of following us, I'd like to point out I've seen a lot of deer out on the trail. And there's nothing I like better than fresh killed venison. And me being as hungry as I am, well, I might just mistake one of you for stew fixin's. And that'd be a shame now, wouldn't it?" He reeled his horse around and followed Ki to the stables.

As Ki passed by Chan Pei, a thought struck him. He turned to the tall Chinese. "Let me see that dagger," he demanded.

The man showed an expressionless face and ignored the request.

"I have seen a dagger like that once before, in San Francisco," Ki thought out loud. "A Tong lord wore it on his belt."

The Chinaman shook his head slowly.

"Surely you remember the knife I am refering to, Chan

108

Pei. A few minutes ago you were all too willing to stick it into my back."

Chan Pei reddened. "When you see that blade again it will be but briefly, as it slits open your throat."

Ki laughed harshly. "Boys should not play with sharp knives. They may get cut."

"Laugh now, barbarian. Soon your voice will be choked by the flow of your vile blood."

Ki wasn't sure why he continued to taunt Chan Pei. It wasn't necessary to see the knife. The elaborate handle of the dagger was sticking out from the man's pocket, and Ki had seen enough of the stylized dragon's head to identify the origin of the weapon. But he felt compelled to push Chan Pei further, to grind the cocky man's nose into the dirt—if not literally, then figuratively.

"You are a coward, Chan Pei." Saying that, Ki shot out his right hand and tweaked the Chinaman's nose. His move took Chan Pei totally by surprise. But when the shock wore off, Chan Pei would be ready to fight. Ki lowered himself into a horse-stance and had his hands up and open.

Chan's eyes burned with anger, but his voice was calm. There was even the faintest trace of a smile at the corner of his lips. "It is you who are the coward, barbarian. You fight bravely against men trained only to wrestle animals. You would not fare so well against a man trained in combat—against a warrior." Chan lowered himself into a fighting stance, and with deliberate precision flexed each finger into the shape of a powerful claw.

"It takes more than a fancy posture to prove mastery in an art," Ki said condescendingly. But despite his words he was impressed. To one with experience, a master of an art can be spotted almost immediately. The fluid movements, the precise position, the conservation of effort all spoke well of Chan Pei's skill in the martial arts. But Ki was not going to admit that.

Chan Pei, though, knew he was good. He didn't need a compliment to bolster his ego. "If you have any skill, barbarian, you know I am your superior. If you are more foolish than I realize, you will learn the hard way."

"From one who lets others fight his battles, brave words come cheap," Ki taunted.

Chan Pei relaxed. "There will be no fight, barbarian. I do not wish to bloody my hands or soil my clothes. But you will learn your lesson." He moved his open hand next to Ki's, and rested against it lightly, back to back. "It is called 'sticky-hand.'"

"I have heard of it," Ki answered. "It is a training exercise."

"It is a way of training disrespectful upstarts," Chan Pei said sharply. "It teaches them respect for their masters."

"A very important lesson to learn," Ki agreed.

"The object is to control your opponent's hand with your own, while never losing contact. You may attempt a strike at the time of your choosing. Begin."

The duel began slowly, with each man feeling out the other. A gentle push here, a feint there. It looked simple; often there was no visible action at all, just two arms extended, hands open, resting against each other. But looks were deceiving.

"It is a contest of subtleties, barbarian. I am surprised you are capable of understanding this." Chan used his words as a distraction. As he spoke he pivoted his wrist and slid it under and over Ki's hand. Pushing Ki's wrist out of the way, he moved his hand in to strike.

Ki reacted quickly to the change of pressure and rolled his own hand with Chan Pei's. They had now reversed position, and Ki moved his hand towards Chan's face.

The Chinaman was surprised that Ki had thwarted his attack, but reacted equally as fast. Once again the two hands were resting against each other, seemingly immobile. The whole parlay had not taken much more than a second.

Chan Pei laughed. "You learn fast, barbarian. That is good. It is always more pleasing to beat a good opponent."

So saying, he once again initiated an attack, which had no better results than the first.

"With an exercise that requires so much concentration I am amazed that you use your mouth so much," Ki remarked. "Or is that part of your strategy?"

"I need no strategy against the likes of you," Chan hissed.

Ki noticed Chan's jaw tighten. The man was getting increasingly frustrated with each blocked attack. This gave Ki an immediate sense of gratification. But Ki did not know how long he could keep the upper hand. Though he had seen this 'sticky-hand' before, doing it was a totally different experience. He was a novice at it, while Chan Pei was an adept. In the end Ki would lose, unless he could force Chan into a costly mistake.

The contest demanded a great amount of strength and endurance. Small, precise movements required more effort than larger, broad sweeps of the arm. The one error Chan might make would be one of underestimating his opponent's stamina. It wouldn't be too hard to trick Chan into being overconfident. If Ki feigned weakness Chan Pei would be all too quick to believe it. Ki could lure him in, then strike on the counterattack.

Ki was going to set it up slowly, but Chan was an observant opponent. Ki gave a little sigh, and Chan tensed, looking for an opening. When Ki relaxed his hand just momentarily and stretched out his fingers, Chan sensed victory. He moved swiftly, but Ki was ready with a block and a strike. But Ki had also made the mistake of underestimating his opponent. Chan Pei was fast—fast enough to recover and block Ki's attempt.

Chan Pei was also an aware fighter. He realized almost instantly that he had been duped, that Ki had tricked him with the ploy of being tired. This angered him; Ki could read it in his eyes. So although the actual ruse had not worked, Ki might still reap the benefits. He watched the rage build up in Chan. Soon it would reach the point where it would cloud his thinking, and mar his fast reflexes. One mistake and Ki would have him.

"Let's go, friend. I ain't got all day to watch you play patty cake," Mercer called impatiently from his horse.

Thinking Ki to be distracted, Chan Pei struck. His hand shot out right towards Ki's jugular. So intent was he that he forgot the rules of the game, forgoing the need to maintain hand contact. With a mighty swing he had knocked Ki's hand away, and was just inches from clawing Ki's throat, when Ki's other hand sprang up and caught Chan's claw. Ki's hand closed, his grip tightening.

For a moment, it seemed a stalemate. But as Ki's hand enclosed Chan's and his powerful fingers dug into the back of Chan's hand, Ki could see the signs of pain show in the Chinaman's face. The muscles tensed, his jaw gritted. Ki continued the viselike pressure; only the strength in the Chinaman's fingers kept them from breaking. But still the pain must have been excruciating, and Chan Pei uttered not a sound.

But something had to give. It was no surprise when Chan's free hand moved to the dagger. Ki's foot was in motion before the dagger cleared its sheath.

Ki's foot exploded in Chan's groin. With a cry of pain, the Chinaman collapsed to the dirt, both hands gripping at his testicles. He stared up at Ki through watery, tear-filled eyes. "You are a dead man, barbarian," he gasped weakly.

★

Chapter 11

"I think you got some explaining to do, friend," Mercer said as he and Ki rode side by side out of town. "An' you can start with your name."

"The name's Ki."

"And you're not just passing through, are you, Ki?" Mercer said pointedly.

Ki wasn't going to deny it, but he didn't answer immediately. He wanted to take a minute to sort out where he stood, and how best to proceed.

Mercer misread his hesitation. "You seemed awfully chummy with those coolies . . ."

Ki laughed. "Chummy's not the word."

And considering you was asking innocent questions about the Double C just a few minutes ago, it's near amazing you knew Tsen-ti was the foreman."

"A lucky guess?" Ki said with a smile. But then he proceeded to tell Mercer everything, including the original suspicion that Mercer was behind Scott's shooting.

"Figures the old coot would try to pin it on me, but what makes you so sure I didn't do it?" he asked Ki.

"Nothing," Ki answered frankly.

Mercer made a face and was about to protest when Ki cut him off. "Except I don't think it's in your nature."

"That's more like it, friend."

"And I don't think you knew Scott was selling his outfit. I also think you knew nothing about him being shot."

"It came as a surprise to me," Mercer affirmed.

Ki looked thoughtful. "Which leaves me confused. Scott thinks he was shot to prevent the deal from being closed. That means the ambusher had to know about the sale. Until I know who Scott told, the trail goes nowhere."

"Hammel, for one, knew."

Ki turned to the rancher. "Is he the type that would spread it around?"

Mercer shook his head. "He barely got around to telling me. If it weren't for the questions you were asking, I still wouldn't know."

"Maybe it has nothing to do with the selling of his ranch," Ki mused.

"Might be just a coincidence," Mercer agreed, though his tone was skeptical.

Ki laughed. "I don't believe it either. Did Scott have any enemies?"

"Besides me?" Mercer shook his head. "None that I know of."

"Why don't you two get along?" Ki asked outright.

The rancher shrugged. "'Cause he's mean an' ornery, an' just as soon rip a polecat apart with his bare teeth. Why I once heard it told that Gerald Scott. . . ." He trailed off once he saw that Ki was not overly amused. "It may seem one-sided of me," he continued seriously, "but I don't like

114

the man because he is mean, and never gives me a minute's peace."

"It doesn't seem like Scott, but I have heard the things he says of you," Ki agreed.

"Basically, he resents anyone else coming into his valley and raising stock. He was here first, and anyone else, well, they just don't belong."

"He doesn't seem to have any animosity towards anyone else," Ki remarked.

"Sodbusters are no competition; neither are the handful of other ranches. They're all one-pasture ma-and-pa outfits."

"The Lazy M is the only other large outfit?"

"You got it, Ki."

"I hope you don't mind me saying this, but you're hardly in the same league."

Mercer chuckled. "The truth don't bother me—much. But how do you know?"

"I've done some looking for myself. Your land's hardly prime grazing."

The rancher nodded. "And I think that galls the old man even more. Scott came here and bought up all the good land. Figured what he didn't own was hardly worth having. Then I come along a few years later, bought up the land he passed over—for a song, mind you—and made a reasonable go of it."

"He still has the best spread in the valley," Ki objected. "Why should he care that you're succeeding?"

"It must stick in his craw like a dry thistle," Mercer said with a smile.

"I don't see why. There's no real competition."

"It ain't the competition at all. It's his fool pride. He looked at my corner of the valley and saw dry, rocky land. I looked at it and saw possibility. Dig a few wells, a couple of windmills, and it might work. It'll never support five thousand head, but I'm doing all right. And that old coot

115

just hates to be proved wrong. It must choke him every morning," he said with a chuckle.

"What about the rustling?" Ki asked bluntly. "Why does he accuse you of that?"

Mercer smiled. "I reckon I'm a tad aggressive come spring round-up. I don't have a big outfit, with thirty men, Ki. Soon as the ground thaws I'm out on the range with my hands, an' we stay out there till all my calves are branded."

"Roping in the mavericks."

"I won't deny it," Mercer said flatly. "Same as any other good rancher, Scott included. I just get a jump on 'em. I have to. With only four or five hands, it takes me three times as long to work my range."

"But I can see why Scott gets sore. With you throwing a long rope, you must grab up a lot of his calves."

"I won't take no offense, Ki, 'cause I know you don't mean what you just said," Mercer said sternly. Then his tone softened and he continued. "I usually don't get more than a few of his stock. Mostly by honest mistake. I think it barely keeps me ahead of what he grabs of mine."

Ki looked surprised. "I guess there are two sides to every coin."

Mercer nodded. "Think about it, Ki. Scott has the better pastures. Greener, more protected. Come early spring a good chunk of my herd wanders on to Double C land. Even dumb critters ain't gonna search out dry, rocky slopes. It's not a two-way exchange."

"Makes sense," Ki said.

"If I don't start roundup early, I lose half my newborns to the Double C. But I don't call them rustlers."

"Ever try to explain that to Scott?"

"Not in the past couple of years. Just falls on deaf ears."

"Hmmm. Back in the saloon you said something about Scott being too dumb to realize his own men were cheating him. Got any proof?"

The rancher shook his head. "Just plain horse sense. Scott keeps bellyachin' he's losing stock. Well, I know I'm not taking any. Neither are any of the other ranchers."

"How do you know that?"

"First, you just know." Mercer smiled. "Secondly, all the other small ranchers are struggling. If they were stealing from the Double C they'd all be sitting pretty. And they're not."

"They could be taking just a few head."

"Like I said, Ki, I don't take no offense hearing you talk like that. But if the wrong fellow hears you accuse him like that . . ." He shook his head. "Well, I just don't want to be responsible."

Ki tried to control his smile. "I'll try and remember that. But it could be happening."

Mercer was shaking his head. "It could be, but that wouldn't even come close to the figures Scott's always screaming about."

"Interesting."

"Yup. You could restock all the small spreads with what Scott loses a year."

"And you think it's his own men."

"Like I said. Just plain horse sense. When you have losses like that year after year, I'd check the tally sheets, then get myself a new foreman."

"You might be right, Mercer," Ki agreed. It did seem that Scott gave a lot of responsibility to Tsen-ti and the crew for the running of the ranch. Ki considered the possibility in silence, wondering how everything else fit in if in fact the crew was embezzling from their boss.

Ki brought his horse to a stop. "Is there any way to cut across to the Double C, or do I have to go back to town?"

"If you know the way, the most direct route is through those hills." Mercer pointed to their left. "But you won't get there before sundown."

"I should get back and tell Je—my boss—the crew might be stealing from Scott." For some reason unknown even to himself, Ki had balked at letting Mercer know he worked for Jessie.

117

"Take it from me, Ki: As an owner, I'd rather have my man arrive the next day, safe, than have him ride through the night over rough terrain, and risk his losing his horse in a bad fall."

Ki said nothing, but looked undecided. Mercer continued. "Is your boss one of those syndicate men that sits behind a desk all day, or does he know something of the business?"

"She," Ki said flatly. There was no reason to hide it, and Ki wasn't purposely going to avoid it. "I work for a woman. Jessica Starbuck."

"Well, if that don't beat all," Mercer whistled softly. "Must be a real battle-axe."

"She's a tough woman," Ki agreed. "Most people don't want to cross her."

"Her husband die off and leave her holding the reins?" Mercer wondered.

"She's never been married," Ki informed him truthfully.

"No wonder. Who'd want a crusty old nag . . .?"

Ki didn't know exactly why Mercer had formed that opinion of Jessie, but recalling how Mercer had pulled his leg in the saloon, Ki saw no reason to correct the rancher. "She's not so bad, if you can get on her good side."

"And what side is that?" Mercer laughed uproariously at his little joke. He stopped shortly, and looked serious. "Still, does she know anything about ranchin', or does she buy as an investment?"

"She knows something of cattle," Ki answered. "She was raised on a Texas ranch. She can ride and rope better than most," he added proudly.

"What's it like working for a lady? Do men respect her?" Mercer asked seriously.

"I can't imagine working for anyone else. I've been with the Starbuck outfit since I came to this country," Ki informed him. "Most of her crew feel the same."

"That so?"

Ki nodded. "She's quite a special person."

118

"She must be to keep hard-ridin' men in line."

"She does more than just keep them in line. She really commands loyalty. Most ranchers could learn plenty from her."

"Then I'll be pleased to have you as neighbors."

Ki grinned. "Matter of fact, a few years working the range side by side and you'll know more about calves than a mother cow."

"I'll be looking forward to meeting this gal," Mercer said with a smile.

Ki returned the smile. "I hope I'll be around when you do," he said quite honestly.

"Then that just about settles it."

"What?"

"You'll be spending the night at the Lazy M. I'm sure your Miss Starbuck won't have you ruining a company horse."

Ki still had not made up his mind.

Mercer continued. "Besides, it may not be safe cutting across the range at night."

"Why?" Ki asked with interest.

"We don't know where Chan Pei and his bunch are. They could be bivouacked out there somewhere. And he might still be fuming mad. I pulled you out back there, but I won't be around next time."

"Oh, I wasn't aware of your help," Ki said with interest.

"Sure. That Chinaman was moving in for the kill. Someone had to do something."

"And that someone was you."

Mercer nodded. "By rushing you along, I thought it'd put an end to the match. Course it did, but not exactly the way I had it planned."

Ki laughed. "Inadvertently you did help. Chan Pei thought I was distracted and made his final move. . . . But what makes you so positive he was moving in for the kill, as you put it?"

"Was plain as daylight. You could read it in his eyes."

Ki said nothing, but he found himself respecting Tom Mercer all the more.

A short time later they arrived at the Lazy M ranch house. "It's not much, but it's home. Take any bed in the bunkhouse. I'll have a hot meal cooking in no time," Mercer promised.

After a meal that was surprisingly tasty, Mercer went to a pine cabinet and pulled out a bottle of whiskey. He poured two glasses and offered a toast: "To new friends, whether they be passing drifters, or new neighbors." Ki hesitated a moment before picking up the glass. "Go on," Mercer urged. "It's quality drink—imported. And not from Mexico, either," he added with a smile.

Ki picked up the glass. "To new friends," he said and took a gulp.

The two men talked a bit more before turning in for the night. As Ki headed out the door, Mercer stopped him. "And Ki, thanks for helping out a stranger this afternoon. I hate to think what might have happened if—"

"Don't mention it, Tom. It was my pleasure."

Ki awoke early the next morning, but apparently not all that early. When he stepped out of the bunkhouse, Mercer was already on top of the windmill beginning his work day.

"Mornin', Ki," Mercer called from his perch. "There's some hot coffee on the stove, and some not so hot biscuits in the pan."

"I'll hold awhile," Ki said as he walked to the base of the twenty-five-foot tower. "Need a hand?"

Mercer shook his head. "I'm just changing the leather on the top check."

"Pulling rods goes faster with two men."

The rancher smiled. "So you know something about windmills?"

"About all there is to know," Ki said frankly. "Don't

most top hands?" he added with a smile.

It wasn't that great a boast. Windmills were simple, uncomplicated pieces of machinery that were standard on the ranches and farms of Texas and the dry plains region.

They consisted of three major parts: the tower, the head and the hole. The tower was the easily recognized structure that dotted many a landscape. On the top sat the fan, which caught the wind; the head, which had gears and bearings that would convert the rotary movement of the fan to vertical, up-and-down strokes; and the tail, which was used not only for balance, but to keep the fan pointed to the wind.

In the ground a large casing and a smaller, hollow pipe were sunk down to the waterline. Within the pipe, wood rods ran up to the platform and connected to the head. At the water level these rods had leather checks and ball valves. The bottom check and valve would let water into the pipe, but would not let it out; the top check worked the reverse, letting the water out into the reservoir. When wet, the leather would form a tight seal, and with each up-and-down stroke of the rods, suction would be created and water would pump.

"Back in town you offered a meal and a place to lay my head, and I promised a good day's work," Ki said as he started to climb the scaffolding.

"And I reckon you always keep your word."

Ki nodded. "I ate your food last night, so now you're stuck with me."

"Welcome aboard," Mercer said as he helped Ki over the top.

"How deep is it?" Ki inquired.

"Only about thirty feet."

"Then we'll be finished by noon."

"If it's only the top leather," Mercer cautioned. If the bottom valve had to be changed the rods, once they were pulled out, would have to be lowered back into the hole to engage the bottom check, then removed again. It was at least twice the work. Sometimes the rods wouldn't catch the bottom valve easily and the chore became a frustrating and tedious job.

"There's only one way to tell," Ki answered as he took hold of the first wooden shaft.

They were lucky. The top leather proved to be worn and ill-fitting, and after replacing it with a piece custom-made by the town saddlemaker, the pump was again working well.

The last rod was just being put back in place when they saw a rider approach. Ki knew it was Jessie. There was no mistaking her statuesque form. He could hardly contain his smile at what he expected would happen.

A few minutes later she reined in under the windmill. "Howdy ma'am," Mercer called down to her. "What can I do for you?"

"I'm looking for Thomas Mercer."

"This must be my lucky day," he whispered to Ki. Then he started down the scaffold. "I'm Tom Mercer," he announced halfway down the tower.

"I'm Jessica Starbuck. I just bought the Double C, Mr. Mercer."

Mercer did a quick double-take, his eyes nearly bulging out of their sockets. His jaw dropped and he started to say something when his feet got tangled up and he slipped from the wooden framework.

With a thump, he landed hard on his back. Jessie slid down from her horse and rushed over to him. "Are you all right, Mr. Mercer?"

The rancher opened his eyes and stared up into Jessie's sparkling green eyes. "I done died an' gone to heaven. The good Lord's taken pity on old Tom Mercer. . . ."

"I hardly think so, Mr. Mercer," she said, barely controlling her smile. But that only encouraged him more.

"The angels are smiling down upon me," he muttered wistfully.

"I'm the new owner of the Double C. You'll find me rather less than angelic . . ."

Mercer raised his head slightly, and caught sight of Ki grinning broadly. The rancher's eyes twinkled mischievously. "Starbuck . . . bought up Scott's spread . . ." he began, feigning confusion. Then the fog seemed to clear. "Why, yes! You're the old bag Ki works for."

"Pardon . . . ?" Jessie said, not sure she heard right.

Mercer was laughing uproariously. "The battle-axe of a Texas rancher. Rides well, knows cattle, never been married. Ki was telling me all about you."

Jessie blushed, and to cover her embarrassment, turned crossly to Ki. "I don't suppose you'd care to expalin yourself. . . ."

"Excuse me, ma'am. It wasn't his fault," Mercer began hurriedly. "Just a little misunderstanding. He had only the nicest things to say about you. Ain't that true, Ki?" He waited for Ki to answer, but when nothing was said, he continued: "He was trying to have some fun with me, ma'am, and after what I done to him in the saloon the other day, I can't see as how I blame him. But then I turned the tables on him. Only I didn't mean to cause you no offense."

"You're not talking a lick of sense, Mr. Mercer," Jessie said patiently.

Mercer picked himself up from the dirt. "After everything Ki has told me about you, I insist you drop the mister."

Jessie stared at him, not knowing how to take his remark.

"He's said nothing but good things about you, Jessica. Said you're a mighty saavy breeder."

"Did he now?"

"And that most ranchers could learn a lot from you. Said your men are mighty pleased to be workin' for you, too."

"Did he . . . ?" Her anger seemed to be passing.

"Only thing, ma'am, was he failed to say what a beautiful woman you are." Again Jessie blushed, but this time it was a less awkward situation. "An' I just naturally assumed a woman of your abilities and qualifications had to be, ah, somewhat older."

Jessie let out a laugh. She had experienced that before, many times. "Ki, you can thank your friend for pulling you out of the water."

"I suppose I could," Ki said as he hopped down off the scaffolding. "But seeing as how he threw me in in the first place, I'll call it even."

"Even," agreed the rancher. "Now let's go on up to the house, and I'll fetch you something cool to drink, Jessie, and you can tell me what brought you out this way."

"In a minute," she said politely. She turned towards Ki, her tone serious. "There's been an accident, Ki. Tsen-ti is dead." Jessie's voice softened. "I thought maybe you should get back as soon as possible—for Ling Ling."

Without a word, Ki strode off to the barn. A moment later he trotted out on the back of the roan, and was soon a fading cloud of dust.

Chapter 12

Ki held her close to him. He could not find the right words, so he remained silent, hoping that his touch alone would offer some comfort to the grieving Ling Ling.

Eventually Ling Ling lifted her head from his shoulder. She took him by the hand and led him into the kitchen. "Sit down, Ki. You must be hungry. I'll get you something to eat."

"Don't worry about me, Ling Ling," Ki said softly.

"It's no worry," she answered.

"I don't have much of an appetite," he said, even though he had had nothing to eat since last night's meal.

Ling Ling stood there motionless, then rushed into his arms. "Just hold me tight."

Ki obeyed, holding her with one muscular arm and stroking her hair gently with his other hand. When he felt her relax against him, he squeezed her even tighter. "How's Tommy?" he asked after a short while.

Ling Ling pulled her head back enough to stare into Ki's eyes. She shrugged her shoulders. "He's been keeping to himself." She sniffed loudly. "Maybe you could have a talk with him. He thinks so much of you."

"I'll see if it will help."

Ling Ling moved away. "Go now, Ki," she said softly. "He's been sulking all day." She squeezed both his hands, "Thank you, Ki."

Ki found Tommy in the barn. The boy was lying against a bale of hay, staring off into the distance. Ki sat down next to him. He was thinking of what to say when it dawned on him that he didn't know Tommy's religious background. Was he a converted Christian, a Confucian, a Taoist, or a Buddhist? Ultimately, Ki decided it mattered hardly at all. Whether Tommy's beliefs taught him there was a heaven, an afterlife, or a transmigration of the soul, right now all he was feeling was a deep grief and a sense of loss. Abstract philosophical and religious doctrines would do little to comfort him.

"You will always remember and respect the memory of Tsen-ti," he said softly.

"I know," Tommy said bitterly.

Ki shook his head. "But you will cloud that memory if you fill your life with angry sorrow."

"I can't help it, Ki."

"Tommy, you cannot change what has been done. And someday soon you will find yourself grieving less."

"No I won't," the boy said defiantly.

Ki smiled to himself. "That would not make Tsen-ti proud."

"I . . . I . . . " the boy faltered.

"He would not be happy knowing you spend your days inside a dark barn."

"But I don't want to do anything else," Tommy whined.

"I just want to sit here and be left alone."

"That is no way to honor Tsen-ti."

"It's not honor, it's punishment," Tommy said enigmatically.

"I don't understand."

"It's my fault he died, Ki." The boy was fighting back the tears.

"Tell me what happened." Ki had not found the courage to ask Ling Ling. When he saw her saddened, tear-streaked face, his only desire was to hold her and try and comfort her. He had no wish to discuss the grim details. At the time, the how of Tsen-ti's death seemed unimportant. But now he wanted to know. Talking about it might also help Tommy.

"You mean how he died?" Ki nodded, and Tommy continued. "He was dragged by his horse."

Tommy shrugged. "Maybe he hit his head on a branch, or his horse stumbled, or, who knows . . . ?"

"Was he a good rider?"

"The best!" the boy answered quickly. "I don't care what Chan Pei says."

Ki felt an odd sensation travel up the back of his spine. Involuntarily, he stiffened. "What does Chan Pei say?"

"That my uncle roped more than he could handle."

Ki noted that Tommy referred to Tsen-ti as his uncle, though technically he wasn't. "What was Uncle doing?"

"Roping a mustang."

"And he got caught up in the rope, fell, and was dragged by his horse," Ki said, completing the scenario.

"That's what must have happened," Tommy agreed weakly.

"No one saw?" Ki felt suspicion growing within him.

Tommy shook his head. "He was out by himself. He left in the middle of the night. I wish I knew how it happened, Ki. Uncle was too good to let himself get dragged like that."

"Accidents happen even to the best riders, Tommy. There's no getting around that." What Ki said was true, but ever since the mention of Chan Pei, Ki was beginning to have his doubts.

"I know that, but—"

"Now why do you blame yourself? Why is it your fault?" Ki asked, getting back to the boy's problem.

"He went out to rope me a mustang."

"Who knew that?" Ki tried to ask the question as innocently as possible.

"Everyone," the boy answered. "He told everyone he'd be back by morning with my new horse." Tommy's voice started to get thick as he choked back the tears.

Ki decided to deal with his suspicions later. Now it was time to rid the boy of his unnecessary guilt. "Tommy, when you rushed into the burning barn, you knew it was dangerous, right?"

"Of course."

"You knew you might die trying to save the horses."

"I tried not to think about that," the boy said bravely.

"But something terrible might have happened . . ."

"It almost did," Tommy said gravely.

Ki smiled warmly and put his arm around the boy's shoulder. "We were lucky," Ki agreed. "But if something did happen would you want Ling Ling and Tsen-ti to mope around all day, and blame themselves?"

"No, of course not, I'd want them to—" Tommy stopped instantly as the analogy hit home.

Ki could see the realization in the boy's eyes. He stood up, then, offering a hand to Tommy, he helped the boy to his feet. "I think your aunt is a little worried."

"I'll go talk to her soon."

"She could use some comforting," Ki prodded gently.

Tommy nodded. "I'll go now."

"Good."

As Tommy reached the door, Ki called out to him. "Where's Tsen-ti's horse now?"

Tommy pointed to the large bay in the far stall. "That one, there."

"And is that his saddle?" Ki asked of the one that straddled the stall wall.

Tommy nodded and continued up to the house. But two steps later he turned back to the barn. "Thanks, Ki," he said sincerely.

Ki smiled and waved. He stood and waited a moment, watching as the boy walked off. Then he turned to Tsen-ti's horse, and the smile faded from his face.

Ki had to assume that the story was true; that Tsen-ti was out roping wild horses. And that his body was found, dragged to death. But that left a lot of gray areas, a lot of room for foul play.

Ki studied the horse carefully, checking the legs for cuts or bruises that might be an indication of a fall. He found no telltale marks, but that proved nothing, either way. The saddle, though, was another story.

What had happened to Tsen-ti was not out of the ordinary. Many a rider often found himself in trouble at the wrong end of a roped animal, but it did not always end so tragically. An animal, a horse, or a rope, would sometimes be lost. A rider could be unhorsed, even bruised badly. But if caught up in the rope, or hung up in the stirrup, there could be serious repercussions. If a man was to die, that's how it would happen.

There were two kinds of roping methods. One was the hard and fast method, where the rope was tied securely to the saddle horn. Then there was the dally method, where the rope was held loose, and dallied or wound around the saddlehorn. Each method had certain advantages and disadvantages. And when the roper got in trouble, the two styles also tended to cause different injuries.

With the dally method, because the rope was loose, it was a simple matter to disconnect from the source of trouble. If a rider did rope a brute that was causing more trouble than it was worth he would simply unwind the rope from the horn. That could mean the loss of a rope, but that was always cheaper than sustaining a serious injury. The danger with the dally was that a finger could get caught in the quickly tightening rope. The tension could often snap off a thumb. Many an old-time dally man was missing a part of his thumb. It was common knowledge that if you were going to dally you'd best learn to do it right. Still, an experienced dally man rarely found himself in serious danger.

The hard and fast ropers, though, when confronted with a problem, would have only one way out—snap the rope. The shorter grass ropes they chose to use would enable them to do just that with a quick turn of their horse. But if the critter on the other end of the lasso charged the rider, or moved with the horse, sometimes creating enough tension to snap the rope was difficult. A wild horse or an angry steer could keep enough slack in the rope to cause a serious situation. In cases like that, an unfortunate rider could become tangled up in his rope.

Mistakes made by a dally man might cost him a finger, but a mistake by a hard and fast roper could cost him his life. There were always exceptions, but not often.

Ki wondered what method Tsen-ti had used. It was no secret. One look at the saddle gave him his answer.

Tsen-ti was a dally man. The saddlehorn was large and covered with rawhide to help grip the coils of rope. The saddle was also a single-fire rig, as opposed to a Texas rig that had two cinches and was favored by every hard and fast man. He didn't even have to ask Tommy what kind of rope Tsen-ti used. He was positive it would be a reata, a long, braided rawhide lasso.

Ki left the barn slowly. The knowledge that Tsen-ti was murdered was troubling him. It was news he did not want to share with Ling Ling, at least not until he could name the killer. And although he had a likely suspect, he had no proof, and no motive. It was another question, but now Ki was determined to find an answer, and soon.

As he stepped up to the porch, Tommy came out of the house. Ki was suddenly taken with an idea. "Tommy, could you do me a favor?"

"Anything you want, Ki," the boy responded eagerly.

"Could you find out— but quietly— which hands were out riding the line last night?"

"You mean the night of my uncle's accident?" Tommy said shrewdly.

Ki nodded.

"I already know." Ki looked surprised. Tommy smiled and explained. "I know where every horse is, every day. And you can bet where a horse is, his rider ain't too far off," he said proudly.

"Do you know where Chan Pei was?" Ki asked, getting right to the heart of the matter.

"He left for town early that morning."

"But didn't he just get back from there?"

Tommy shrugged and looked confused. "Day before he was out riding the line with some other hands. . . ."

So nobody knew about Chan Pei's little run-in with Mercer, Ki suddenly realized. "Any idea why he went?" Ki wondered aloud.

"Said he had to send off a telegram."

"And who found your uncle?"

Again Tommy shrugged. "Lee was the first to see the horse. He was just heading over the north rise when he spotted Chestnut heading for the barn. They followed her tracks and a few miles away found Uncle."

"Why did you think Tsen-ti might have hit his head on a limb?" Ki asked abruptly.

"He had this big gash on his forehead." Tommy pointed to right below the hairline. "I didn't want to look, but I had to, once."

"Thank you, Tommy," Ki said as he started into the house.

"Do you think someone killed Tsen-ti?"

The frankness of the question startled Ki. He was about

131

to deny it; then looking into the boy's face, he decided to trust him. "I don't know who or why, but I don't think your uncle died an accidental death."

"Ki, I want to help you find the man who murdered my..."

Ki smiled. "The best way you can help is by keeping your eyes and ears open and your mouth shut."

Tommy nodded. "I'll let you know if I hear or see anything."

"Good." Ki was still concerned that the boy might get himself into trouble, so he added a final word of caution. "Remember, as long as the killer doesn't suspect we're onto him, we have a chance of catching him."

That night Ki held Ling Ling close. Though their lovemaking was very enjoyable, it was not as passionate as the other nights. Ki guessed the secret he was keeping from her and the sorrow at hand put up barriers that interfered with the total emotional and physical union of their bodies. How could he share with her completely when he held back? How could he be thoroughly relaxed when he kept from her his knowledge that Tsen-ti was murdered? But he couldn't mention it. He couldn't bring himself to cause her additional anguish. He reasoned that if she knew, her efforts to find the killer would only impede his investigation. But he had a feeling that reason had little to do with it. Basically, he knew he would do anything to shelter Ling Ling from bodily or emotional harm.

Ling Ling must have felt a difference too. She apologized for her lack of enthusiasm. "My grief still clings heavy to my heart, dear Ki," she said softly.

Ki kissed her forehead gently.

"It is not that I love you any less," she continued.

"If you had a heart of rock, Ling Ling, if you did not feel the sorrow, I couldn't love you as much as I do," Ki answered.

She raised up on her elbow, and peered into his face, tracing with her finger the narrow beam of moonlight that fell against his cheek. "But my heart should be yours, and yours alone."

"It will be," Ki said confidently.

"And we should have no secrets."

Ling Ling's weight pressed down on him. Ki shifted uneasily. "We won't." He never once suspected that perhaps it was she that was keeping something from him.

The next day, Ki made the trip to Topanga Falls as fast as possible. He kept to the road and did not stop. By the time he reached town, his horse was exhausted. That didn't matter. If he needed a fresh mount he would rent one from the livery.

He wanted to check up on Chan Pei immediately. He wanted to know if the man really had been in to send a telegram. On the slim possibility that he had, Ki wanted to know to whom the message was sent.

He walked straight to the telegraph office. Inside, the assistant telegrapher, a tall, lanky youth, sat at the counter. He smiled as Ki entered.

"Help you, mister?"

Ki nodded. "Yesterday, I sent someone in to get off a telegram. We must have missed each other on the trail. Chan's always in a hurry; likes to take short-cuts," Ki said with a smile. "I'd just like to make sure he made it in to the office."

"You got the address?"

Ki seemed to ignore the question. "He was a tall Chinese fellow, shoulder-length hair. . . . "

The youth smiled. "Built like you."

"My cousin," Ki said.

"Was in here yesterday morning," the assistant confirmed.

"I'd like to see the message," Ki began. "Just so I know he got it right."

The youth shook his head. "Can't rightfully do that, mister."

Ki dug into his pocket and pulled out a handful of silver

133

coins. He stacked two silver dollars on the counter.

The youth's eyes twinkled. "Course if you can tell me the message I could tell you if that's the way the telegram read."

Ki was adding another coin to the stack when a pasty, elderly man toting a large beer belly waddled out of the back office.

"What's the dawdling?" he croaked impatiently. "If you're sending a telegram let's have it. If not, be on your way."

Ki's hand moved quickly to cover the coins. The youth looked disappointed, but he had not given up. "I was just checking to see if we got a wire for this gentleman."

"I don't see no gentleman, Evan. All's I see is a dirty coolie."

"The man was just—"

The old telegrapher cut off the youth and addressed Ki sharply. "Your kind keeps forgetting we got laws in this country. You can't come in here and see whatever you damn well want. Why, I have a good mind to send for the sheriff, and have him lock you up." He turned back to his assistant. "Now, boy, get yourself over to the Widow Bushwell and fetch our meal while it's still hot."

"Yes, sir." With an apologetic look to Ki, the assistant left the office.

"I don't suppose you make many friends with that kind of attitude," Ki said dryly.

The man looked him straight in the eye. "I don't need your type for friends."

Ki slid the money off the counter and back into his pocket. It was possible even old Beer Belly would succumb to a bride, but Ki had no desire to fatten the bigot's purse. There were other, cheaper ways of getting the information he wanted.

Later that night, Ki returned to the telegraph office. But he didn't enter through the front door; In fact, he didn't use any door at all. The back room had a window that opened conveniently into the alley.

After prying the latch back with the tip of his *shuriken* Ki quietly slid open the window, and silently climbed into the office.

In his first visit, Ki had seen a bound ledger sitting alongside the telegraph key. He hoped it held a record of all the messages. He walked to the desk, struck a match on the bottom of his boot, and lit the oil lamp. He turned the wick down so that there was just enough light to read by. On second thought, he turned it up bright.

It was not that late. Voices drifted from the saloons and dance halls, and the town sheriff could still be out making his rounds. A dim light coming from the office might raise the curiosity of a passing stranger. With the lamp turned up, someone would simply assume the telegrapher was working late.

Ki grabbed the ledger and scooted down behind the counter; in the brightly lit office he didn't want to risk being spotted.

He started at the back of the book, checked the date, then turned to the front. The newest entries were at the beginning. After a few pages he found the message. It was sent to Wong Import Company, Pier 17, San Francisco. It read:

OBSTACLE ONE REMOVED STOP REQUEST MORE
INFORMATION ON JIBON-REN AND STARBUCK
WOMAN STOP CHAN

Ki started looking for another ledger that would contain the incoming wires, but before he found it he heard a creak come from upstairs. He reached for the lamp and blew it out, but it was too late. He heard footsteps on the floor above, and a minute later he heard the telegrapher's voice call out.

"All right, you varmint. I'm coming down with a shot-

135

gun. I don't want no trouble from you or there'll be daylight streaming through you in more places than the Lord ever intended."

Ki smiled to himself. For all his barking the man was a coward. The telegrapher had no intention of accosting Ki. He was purposely shouting his threats from his upstairs rooms in the hope that by the time he made it down the steps the intruder would be gone.

"I'm coming down now," the old man warned. "My double barrel leading the way."

Ki knew he had time to flee. But he decided to stick around. He wanted to know if Chan Pei had received an answer from the Wong Import Company. He also thought it was time to teach the old blowhard telegrapher a lesson.

Noiselessly he crept to the side of the office where the stairs were. He flattened himself against the staircase and waited. The silence must have proved the coast was clear, and the telegrapher started down the step.

True to the blowhard's word, Ki saw the muzzle of the shotgun appear first. Ki readied himself, waiting as the man walked down another two steps. Then he sprang.

Ki reached out and with both hands grabbed the barrel of the gun and twisted. But the man clung foolishly to the shotgun and wouldn't let go. His strength, though, was no match for Ki's, and as Ki wrenched the gun from his grasp the man went tumbling down the stairs head over heels.

The moment the gun was freed it went off with a loud explosion. The man had filed the action to a hairpin trigger, and the jerk had fired the weapon. The front glass window tinkled to the floor in a thousand pieces.

The telegrapher lay on the floor, stunned. Ki moved closer and a look of terror overcame the man.

"Please, please don't shoot me . . ." he stammered.

Ki wondered if the gun had discharged both barrels or only one. It really didn't matter. Ki certainly didn't need the firearm to control the hapless telegrapher.

The man's fear gave Ki an impulse he would no doubt be ashamed of someday. But right now it seemed fitting.

Ki brought the shotgun up to his shoulder. The man cringed in fear.

"No! Please. I don't have much money, but you can have it all. You can. Anything you want." He started cringing on the floor, desperately trying to wriggle away. Ki kept the gun trained on him. "Anything. Just don't kill me," he continued to wail helplessly.

"A man wouldn't kill a friend, now would he?" Ki said with an ominous grin. "Too bad we're not friends, mister." With that, Ki brought back the hammer of the shotgun.

The man went pale, stiffened slightly, then fainted dead away.

Ki chuckled, carefully uncocked the shotgun, and lowered it to the floor. He was about to resume his search for the incoming logbook when he heard feet running outside in the street.

"Sounded like it came from Grabton's office, sheriff," he heard a voice say.

Ki needed no other warning. He raced to the back window, but as he stepped through he heard a boot tread on broken glass. With the moon as bright as it was, he would be a dead duck if he tried to race down the alley. Ki had no desire to stop a bullet with his back. There had to be another way.

Next to the window was a rain barrel. He stepped up on it, and with a little jump was able to catch hold of the second-story window ledge that was just above. The window was open, and led in to the telegrapher's bedroom. Effortlessly, Ki pulled himself up and into the room.

From underneath the bed he listened to the goings-on downstairs. The sheriff went right to the rear window, then proclaimed softly how the man "musta run like a jackrabbit."

The sheriff then went to the aid of the telegrapher, who

came to stammering about the "Chinese devil."

"Get back to bed, Mr. Grabton. I'll keep one eye on the place."

Grabton muttered his thanks and started to climb back up the stairs. A moment later Ki saw slippered feet approach the bed. He smiled to himself. The telegrapher's ordeal was not quite over yet.

As Grabton approached the bed, Ki reached out, grabbed the man's ankle, and tugged hard. The telegrapher's feet gave way and the man toppled backwards in one smooth motion. Ki scurried out from the bed.

Grabton's eyes went wide. Then, in sheer terror, he fainted.

For a moment Ki was concerned. He didn't want the man to die of shock. He lowered his head to Grabton's chest, and was relieved to hear a weak but steady heartbeat.

Ki decided not to press his luck any further. The sheriff could be back at any moment. Ki didn't have to find the telegram San Francisco wired Chan. He had a feeling he knew how it would read.

Ki slid out the window and walked slowly to the edge of town where he had tethered his horse. Once in the saddle he delayed no longer. He had to get back to the Double C as fast as possible. Other men could be in danger, including Gerald Scott. Even Ling Ling . . .

The inevitable showdown with Chan Pei could wait no longer.

★

Chapter 13

Jessie wanted to get right down to business. She wanted to discuss the accusations Scott had levelled against Mercer, and she wanted to settle the differences between the Double C and the Lazy M. But all Mercer seemed to want to do was apologize for his behavior upon first meeting Jessie.

They were both so intent on their own course of conversation neither one listened to the other. Finally, out of frustration, Jessie raised her voice. "If my neighbor accused me of rustling I'd be right quick to clear my name," she practically screamed. "You hardly seem concerned, Mr. Mercer."

"Because I'm guilty of one and innocent of the other," he answered firmly. "If you'll just listen . . ."

"Go ahead." Jessie conceded.

Mercer explained his behavior and the joke, aimed at

Ki, that backfired. Jessie listened patiently. "And now that we cleared my conscience, what was it troubling you, Miss Starbuck?" he concluded politely.

"Rustling. Encroaching on my land. Fouling my water holes. I won't stand for it. And I won't be intimidated."

"Ki told me as much as," he said under his breath.

"You'll find yourself on the losing end if you cross me or my men," she warned forcefully. She knew she was coming on stronger than necessary, but there was something in Mercer's easygoing good looks that brought it out in her. She was bending over backwards to make certain the man did not think he could charm her easily.

"A battle-axe, all right," he said to himself. But Jessie heard the sentiment, even if she didn't hear the words.

"You may make snide comments now, Mr. Mercer, but you won't find it funny when—"

"Heavens, but you are pretty when you get riled up. Your eyes just light right up."

"I've given you fair warning, Mercer. If I find a Lazy M man on my land I won't be as understanding as Gerald Scott." She turned and started off.

Mercer rushed after her, coming abreast after a few steps. "I'm sorry, Jessie. Really. This is going all wrong. Please come back up to the house and we'll discuss it. Like two mature ranchers."

"I'll give it one more try," Jessie agreed.

"Good. And I promise not to let your good looks interfere."

He said it so seriously and straight-faced, Jessie could not take offense. As a matter of fact, she told herself the very same thing. *I won't let your good looks interfere, either, Tom Mercer.*

Mercer explained the situation to Jessie, telling her just what he told Ki, and then some. It satisfied her, and they soon moved on to other topics.

The two of them sat on the porch and whiled away the

140

hours discussing cattle. Jessie found the rancher's ideas on breeding quite interesting.

"It'd be a boon to your Texas spread to crossbreed your longhorns with our Herefords, but it wouldn't make much sense up here."

"Why do you say that?" Jessie wanted to know.

"Seems like the longhorn's main advantage is a waste in these parts. We ain't got the fever, and with cooler summers than you have in the Panhandle we don't have as many diseases."

"That's a good point, Mercer," Jessie conceded. "But you could do well yourself with a few longhorn bulls."

"Oh?" the rancher said with interest.

Jessie nodded, and a slow smile crossed her lips. "Resistance to disease isn't the longhorn's only good quality."

"They look good over a mantle," Mercer said offhandedly.

"They also fatten easy, even on low-grade grass."

"That so?"

"Yup. And if you don't mind me saying so, you got plenty of low-quality grass here."

Mercer smiled. "You and your friend Ki think alike. He's fond of telling me the same thing."

"Ki's a good cattleman himself," Jessie agreed. "And he doesn't mince words."

"Sounds a little like his employer."

At first Jessie didn't understand. Then she laughed. "I reckon so. But you know, I never think of Ki as an employee. He's part of the family," she said sincerely.

"I think he'd be happy to hear you say that." Suddenly Mercer jumped to his feet. "Damned if I forgot my manners again. Here it is, the day near over, and I'm forgetting my hospitality."

"Hardly."

"First, you must be hungry, and seeing as how it's getting on, I should put you up for the night."

"There's no need, really." Jessie had no desire to head right back to the Double C, but she felt obligated to decline the invitation.

"Nonsense. I had the same trouble with Ki yesterday. It'll be dark before you make it back, and I won't take the chance of something happening to you along the way. My crew is gone. You'll stay in the bunkhouse."

"All right," Jessie agreed. "Why take a chance on an unfamiliar trail?"

"By golly, that's just what I had to tell Ki. I knew you had sense, woman."

Jessie laughed to herself. It wasn't caution so much as Mercer's handsome face and probing eyes that kept her off the trail. And she knew that.

"I'll have dinner ready in no time."

"You just hold it right there, Tom Mercer. If you're going to put me up for the night, I'll earn my keep. Show me to the stove."

"I ain't that bad a cook," Mercer said defensively. "Ask Ki."

"I'm sure you're just fine. But I know how you men cook. Throw anything you have lying around in a big pot, add enough lard, bacon fat, and beans and you call it stew."

"Well if that don't beat all," Mercer said with a laugh. "I see you've heard of the famous Mercer stew."

Jessie frowned playfully. "I'll bet it's been a while since you had a woman fix you dinner up right." As soon as the words left her mouth she regretted saying them. Her purpose was much too obvious. But Mercer didn't seem offended. On the contrary.

"Seems to me like you're fishing, woman." Jessie turned scarlet. Mercer continued. "And I'm right flattered."

"You should be. I don't cook dinner for just anybody."

"But to answer your question, it has been a while. When you're busy trying to build up a spread, seems like there's not much time for courtin'. Mind you, though, I ain't been without womanly comforts," he added hastily. "But they usually don't include a home-cooked meal."

Jessie laughed. "I know just what they include, Tom Mercer. And I don't care to hear any more about it," she teased him.

"It's a pity. It's some o' my best story tellin'. Why, once there was this little filly down in—" Jessie gave him another reproachful look, but he had already stopped in mid-sentence. "Some other time, maybe," he said with a huge grin. "Right now, let's get our chow on."

"You'd put the best restaurants of Frisco to shame with a meal like this," Mercer commented happily as he wiped his mouth.

"I'm glad you like it," Jessie said honestly. "I wouldn't want you to think all I know about is cattle."

"Jessie, even if you didn't know a blasted thing, I don't think I'd ever complain. And now I'll do my part."

He went to his favorite cabinet and again pulled out two glasses. Then he started to pour two hefty shots of whiskey.

"I do believe you're trying to get me drunk," Jessie protested half-heartedly.

"Nonsense," Mercer said as he handed her a glass. "I never met a rancher worth his salt who didn't enjoy an after-dinner drink, and a good see-gar," he said with a grin.

"I can't think of a one myself," she agreed.

"But I'm all out of smoke, so this'll have to do by its lonesome," he said as he handed her the glass.

"Just my luck to get short-changed," she said with mock disappointment. "Well here's to new neighbors . . . and Herefords," she said raising her glass.

"To new neighbors, and longhorns. And successful breeding."

As he spoke there was a gleam in his eye that Jessie found extremely attractive. Mercer threw back his glass

143

and emptied its contents. Jessie took a deep breath, then did the same. Almost instantly she felt the warmth of the liquor spread through her body.

Mercer laughed loudly. "Bravo!" He poured himself another shot, then started to refill Jessie's glass.

"I really don't need any more," she said truthfully. She was pretty sure what Mercer had in mind, and she didn't need any further encouragement from the whiskey. After listening to Ki and Ling Ling these past few nights, her desires were easily fueled. Just looking into Mercer's brown eyes aroused her passion. She just hoped Mercer didn't take too long to get around to it. She didn't want to seem too forward, but she didn't know how long she could wait.

"Jessie, you ride, you rope, you know critters," he said with a smile that did more to melt her insides than all the whiskey in the bottle. "Is there anything you can't do as good as a man?"

Jessie smiled back, and was every bit as devastating. "Some things I don't do anything like a man," she said invitingly.

Mercer put down his glass and moved towards her. He sat down on the edge of the table and leaned close, lowering his face to hers. "I can't for the life of me imagine . . ."

"Move any closer, and you'll soon find out."

Mercer put his arm around Jessie's neck and pulled her to him. Their lips met hungrily. There was no hesitation, no shyness; just a burning desire that consumed Jessie. She wanted all of him. Not just his lips, not just his tongue. She wanted to feel the weight of his body against hers, the rocking motion that would quench her desire.

She reached out for him, stroking the back of his neck lightly with her nails. He moaned softly, the vibrations tingling Jessie's lips as their mouths remained pressed together.

Jessie stood up from the chair and leaned against

Mercer. She was momentarily disappointed when their kiss ended, but as she leaned forward, Mercer pressed his head against her bosom. His lips sought her nipples, and as the ruby tips were pressing hard against her shirt, he found them instantly. Even through the cotton material. Jessie could feel the warmth of his mouth. The tease was perhaps a greater turn-on.

And what was good for the goose was good for the gander. Her hand dropped to Mercer's thigh and she ran her fingers up along the inside of his leg. They had only travelled a few inches when they found his hard bulge. Up and down, she traced the outline of his organ, her movements stimulating her desires as much as his.

Mercer stood up and pressed his body against hers. He lowered his head to her neck and nibbled gently on her soft skin. Jessie let out a moan and let her body lean against his. That brought his meaty shaft in contact with her pelvis. Unabashedly she started to grind against him.

Each movement brought with it a new sensation of pleasure. And even though his organ was trapped down his pants leg, each gyration seemed to make it stiffen more. Soon it was rock hard, and giving Jessie more pleasure than she could believe.

Before she realized it Mercer's hand was against her naked breast, kneading her firm flesh.

Her hips started to move with greater urgency, the heat growing inside her loins, the moisture spreading down between her legs.

Mercer dropped both his hands and took hold of her firm, rounded ass. He pulled her tighter against him, not letting her move away—not that she ever would want to.

She could feel his hard bone, digging right against her very spot. It took her breath away, but she continued to move, her pelvis making small quick circles around the length of his shaft. He pulled her even closer to him, holding her mound firmly against his organ.

Did he know the effect that was having on her? Did he know how close she was? How she was teetering on the brink?

Mercer lowered his mouth to her breasts, and sucked her hard red buds into his mouth. She gasped uncontrollably as his hands squeezed her buttocks.

Jessie felt faint. For a moment she didn't think she could keep to her feet. But her pelvic gyrations never ceased. The world could fall apart and still she would continue to press her mound against his now throbbing shaft. She could actually feel it twitching. Her legs, just a moment ago, weak and rubbery, stiffened. Her back muscles tightened and her body arched gracefully. Her breathing stopped for the slightest moment.

Just then, Mercer's teeth pulled gently on her taut nipple.

Jessie let out a scream, climaxed and slumped down to her knees. Her eyes closed, her mind in a fog of pleasure.

When the wave of bliss passed and she opened her eyes her face was resting against Mercer's crotch. She undid his pants, and not so gently yanked then down to his knees. His erect member sprang free, bouncing happily against her face.

Holding it lightly in her hand she ran her tongue up and down its length. Mercer let out a sigh. Jessie smiled. She wanted to excite, then satisfy him, the way he had done her. And the way he was throbbing in her hand she didn't think it would take long.

Holding him firmly at the base she opened her mouth wide and sucked the tip of him into her mouth. Mercer let out a long moan. Slowly she lowered her head, sliding more of him into her wet mouth. His moan turned to a gasp. Then she reversed the process, slipping him from her warm mouth, till only the very tip pressed against her lips. Mercer thrust his hips forward, and Jessie willingly took him back into her mouth.

She set up a steady rhythm, but soon Mercer was thrusting his hips forward at an increasing rate. Jessie smiled to herself. She let go of his shaft and brought her hands around to his ass. She took hold of his muscular buttocks and pressed her face into his crotch. His shaft slid deep into the back of her throat. Mercer let out another long moan. It sent shivers down Jessie's spine. It was then she became aware of her growing desires.

As her fingers traced a pattern lightly along his flesh, Mercer started to buck. Jessie had to consciously relax her throat or she feared she would gag. As her muscles relaxed, his organ seemed to slide even deeper.

Mercer moaned again, and then Jessie realized she could stand no more. She leaned back, letting his manhood drop out of her mouth, then stood up. "I'm sorry, Tom. I wanted to finish you, but I need to have you inside of me, now."

There was an urgency in her voice that could not be ignored, that demanded immediate action. And Mercer's engorged organ could not be denied any longer.

Wordlessly, he swept her off her feet and carried her into the next room. She landed on a soft bed. She wasn't sure how her pants were removed so quickly, but the next thing she realized, Mercer's body was lowering onto her. She felt the brush of his chest against her bosom, then the tip of his manhood prying against her moist folds.

She let out a cry, as his thick shaft entered smoothly and swiftly, burying itself to the hilt.

Her body arched to meet his every thrust. His strokes were powerful and relentless, each one filling her totally. He drove deep into her. With each thrust a slight moan issued from Jessie's lips.

Her whole being, every sense, seemed concentrated in her loins. That certain warm glow began to emanate from her center and encompass her whole body. She knew release was not far off, but unlike her frantic uncontrollable passion in the kitchen now she would lie here luxuriously and bask in the glow. . . .

Jessie closed her eyes and started to lock her knees around his waist, when she suddenly realized she couldn't move her legs. "I'm as helpless as a hog," she cried out. She then understood how Mercer had been able to enter her so quickly; he never took her pants off, he just lowered them to her knees.

Mercer seemed to take no notice of her quandary. He continued to thrust steadily.

"Get my pants off, Tom," she pleaded. "Please . . ."

"Can't stop now," he whispered in her ear.

"I don't like being hog-tied," she said as calmly as possible, but she couldn't quite eliminate the tremor in her voice.

Mercer lifted himself up onto his elbows. "You could have fooled me," he said with a smile.

Jessie wondered if he changed position just so she could see his devilish grin. Well she could be devilish too. "If my pants were off, I could wrap my legs around your neck," she said enticingly.

Unconsciously, Mercer thrust a little harder. "Mmm, sounds good."

"I could squeeze you deep inside of me. . . ."

"We'll have to try that later," he said casually.

Jessie playfully beat her fists upon his back. She then tried to wriggle her pants down below her knees. Her efforts were in vain, but the friction did something marvelous for both of them. Jessie's creamy, soft thighs now entrapped his hard muscle even on his out-stroke, totally encasing every inch of his powerful muscle. He arched his back and lunged into her, again and again.

The world started spinning. Jessie squeezed her eyes shut, the flood of sensation rapidly overpowering her.

She started to buck her hips wildly.

"Easy, gal, or you'll throw me from the saddle," Mercer warned playfully.

But he was so entrenched within her, Jessie had no fear

of losing him. She couldn't have stopped even if she wanted to.

Mercifully, he stayed with her, thrusting hard, burying himself deep.

"Oh yes, ride me." She cried out. "Ride me-EE-EE!"

Drained, exhausted, totally satiated, Jessie collapsed into the soft mattress. She had a vague sense of Mercer sliding off of her. She protested weakly, but doubted if any sound ever left her lips. She could feel the cool air slide gently over her legs as Mercer must have removed her pants.

Then her legs tingled even more as his soft lips ran slowly up the inside of her thigh. Somewhere, somebody moaned. Breathlessly, she anticipated his steady climb to her soft mound. There was another low moan, and Jessie began to suspect that she was the one moaning.

His lips ever so lightly brushed her soft curls. She moaned again, this time very much aware. And then his tongue darted out and pierced her drenched folds like a hot branding iron.

She jerked away and cried out loudly. She rolled quickly to her side, flipping Mercer over in the process.

"Don't you like it?" Mercer wondered, as he lay on his side and stared at her.

"I do, I do," Jessie said, trying to catch her breath. "But it's too much. . . ."

"I'll be gentle."

Jessie laughed. "Gentle's not the problem. I'm much too sensitive. You'll drive me loco."

Judging from his smile, Jessie realized that just might have been the wrong thing to say.

Mercer slid her shirt off her shoulders and pressed his lips to her neck. Slowly, he started kissing his way down over her rounded breasts, hard pointing nipples, and smooth flat stomach.

Jessie was well aware of his objective, though this time

he was working from the top down. She put one hand on each of his shoulders and flattened him to the bed.

"You don't really want me to stop," Mercer said with a grin.

"Oh?" she said with raised eyebrows. He happened to be right, but Jessie wouldn't admit it. Besides, she needed a moment to regain her equilibrium. "How can you be so sure?" she added coolly as she looked down at him. Mercer grinned and shrugged. "Because all your little fillies at the dance halls tell you so?" she said saucily.

"As a matter a fact, yes. But not at the dance halls . . ." he said with a grin.

"Why, I bet they all fight for you. Choose me, Mr. Mercer," she said in a mocking falsetto.

"Funny you should say that."

"I'd like to hear all about it." As she spoke Jessie straddled his shoulders. "Weren't you going to tell me about this little filly . . ."

Mercer smiled and started to speak, but Jessie lowered herself over his warm mouth. Though his lips were moving, his words were unintelligible.

"I don't quite understand, Tom. Could you speak up — o-oh!" She sighed heavily as his tongue once again caressed her.

He was, as promised, very gentle. "It feels like a butterfly," she gasped with pleasure.

She reached behind her, and found his organ hard and thick as a fence pole. She grasped it tightly and began stroking it. Mercer buried his face deeper into her dripping pink petals. She groaned loudly and stroked his shaft faster. That only encouraged his already active tongue.

Jessie felt her knees getting weak. She knew she couldn't stand it much longer. Before long his expert touch would wring another orgasm from her soul.

"This time we're going to finish together," he said in a husky voice. She backed herself off his face, and impaled

150

herself quickly on his tool. In an instant they let out simultaneous groans.

Mercer lunged frantically up into her body, his hips now bucking madly. Jessie took him to the hilt, watching with joy the expression of pleasure that covered his handsome bronze face.

"Be still," she said as his movements became even more intense. "Don't move." She leaned back and lowered her full weight against his thick pole, making his deep thrusting movements difficult.

"But Jessie, we were so clo—ohh." His protest turned to ecstasy as Jessie's inner muscles contracted about his shaft. "I don't know what you're doing, gal, but don't stop!" He moaned again, louder.

Jessie could feel him swell inside her. Her powerful muscles continued to grip him and pump him.

"Don't ever stop," he cried out loudly. "This is like nothing I've ever felt before."

Jessie had no intention of stopping. She closed her eyes and threw back her head, fighting to hold back till Mercer was ready.

She didn't have to wait long. With a cry, he thrust into her, then let loose.

Jessie could feel his warmth spurt deep inside of her. His muscle was contracting strongly. She gasped, then collapsed on top of him as her floodgates opened, and her own sensations wracked her body.

When she opened her eyes she didn't know how much time had passed. It could have been moments or hours. They were still joined together, but Mercer's member was soft and flaccid—not the mighty pole it was before. She enjoyed the feeling of it stuffed snugly into her. Using the very same muscles that had brought them both to ecstasy, she again squeezed his manhood. It quickly came to life, hardening inside of her.

"You're too good for your own sake," Mercer said softly.

His voice surprised Jessie; she thought he was asleep. But there was nothing sleepy in the way he began moving inside of her.

"You may be right," she admitted grudgingly. "I don't know if I could take any more prodding." She slid off of him quickly, before she lost the desire to do so. He sighed disappointedly. "But don't you worry," she said alluringly.

She slid down the bed, till her head was resting against his muscular stomach. Her hand took hold of his shaft, which was once again back to fence-pole proportions. "Don't you have a story to tell me?" she said teasingly as her fingers lightly traced their way along his length.

"A story?" he sounded confused.

"About that young filly in—"

"Oh right," he said with a chuckle. "She was really something. A fine piece of woman flesh."

Jessie lowered her mouth onto his shaft. Mercer moaned contentedly.

She never heard the rest of the story.

★

Chapter 14

Ki burst into the cookhouse. His eyes quickly scanned the crew as they ate their breakfast. "Where is Chan Pei?" he demanded loudly.

There was no response. Ki grabbed the nearest man and lifted him up by the front of his shirt. The rest of the crew jumped to their feet. Ki seemed unconcerned. "I want to know where he is," he repeated, as he shook his captive roughly. "You'll either tell me now or you'll swallow all your teeth."

Ki's ferocity must have kept the others at bay. He could hold off some, but not all of them. He had to press harder while he still had the advantage. He lowered the man to his feet, but still held him firmly with one hand. His other arm cocked back, his hand forming into a threatening fist.

The Chinaman stared in fright. "I don't know! I don't know!"

Ki studied the crew and noticed that all the men that had accompanied Chan to town, the men who were involved in the fight with Mercer, were conspicuously missing. Ki put two and two together. "I'm not afraid of the Tong," he declared boldly. Ki noticed that at his mention of the Chinese secret society a few of the men reacted with surprise.

Hong, the cook stepped forward. He was holding a meat cleaver, though not yet brandishing it as a weapon. Ki stood his ground. "You are a brave but foolish man, *Jibon-ren,*" the cook said.

"The Tong are men, like you, like me."

Hong shook his head. "Sadly, that is not so."

Ki disagreed. "I have battled the Tong before. And I have beaten them. I will beat them again." He saw the disbelief in many of their faces. "It is true. You have heard of Steel Claw. You know of his Tong; you know of his death." Many heads nodded. "It was I who ripped his heart from his body." A few gasped. "Now where is Chan Pei?" he asked for the final time.

Hong shrugged. Ki knew better than to try and strong-arm him. He tried persuasion. "Hong, I do this for your people as well. Did he not kill Tsen-ti? Which one of you will be next?"

"Your hands are not tied, *Jibon-ren.* Perhaps you can defeat Chan Pei. He is no greater an adversary than Steel Claw," Hong said slowly. "But we do not know where he and his men have gone."

Ki sensed it was the truth and left. He walked purposefully up to the house. With each step a strange doubt reared its ugly head.

Ling Ling met him at the front door. "Ki, I was getting worried. I thought you'd be back late last night. I missed you," she added sweetly.

"My horse threw a shoe," Ki explained curtly. "I had to walk most of the distance."

"You must be tired."

"Pack your things, Ling Ling. You and Tommy are going away for a few days."

"What do you mean, Ki? What are you talking about?"

"Please, just do as I say." He didn't raise his voice, but it was as close as he could ever come to yelling at her. He softened his tone somewhat. "Is Scott awake? I must talk with him."

Ling Ling's face went pale. "Don't Ki. You musn't."

Ki looked at her. Suddenly, it became painfully clear.

"Don't look at me that way," Ling Ling pleaded.

"You knew all along," he accused bluntly. She turned her face to the floor. "You knew Chan was rustling stock, that he tried to kill Scott, that he murdered Tsen-ti—"

Her head jerked up. "No!" she screamed in anguish. "It's not true!"

"You did know, Ling Ling. Don't lie to me," Ki said harshly.

"Yes, but not about Tsen-ti. It can't be true," she wailed. But she knew it was.

The initial shock had worn off, and Ki's voice was more gentle, almost weak. "Why didn't you tell me, Ling Ling?"

"You wouldn't understand, Ki. Yes, you would," she added quickly as she looked up into his face. "Come sit down and I'll explain."

She took him by the hand and led him out to the porch. They sat on the top step, holding hands.

"I—we—never thought it would go this far," she began. Then she stopped short. "Let me start at the beginning. All this seems so far away from the crowded streets of Chinatown. And it was, for a brief time. But then the Tong's tentacles reached out even to here. You cannot understand what that means unless you have family back in Chinatown, Ki. The men in the bunkhouse are brave men.

They would gladly fight Chan Pei and the Tong, but their hands are tied."

"Hong used that exact expression," Ki said, almost to himself.

"It is true. They fear for the safety of their mothers and fathers, their sisters, all their relatives that live under the iron rule of the Tong. Every man here has someone back in San Francisco. And the Tong rules that city."

Ki nodded. "I know how the Tong works."

"Then you understand a brave act here will cost them dearly at home."

"But why couldn't you trust me?"

"Trust you to do what, Ki? Turn the other cheek? To let things continue the way they were? You would only make matters worse. And ultimately we and our families in Chinatown would pay the price."

Ki understood her point and nodded. "At least explain things to me now."

Ling Ling nodded. "It started with my brother. As I told you, Zen Mo was something of a local hero, a living legend. His position here lured many Chinese. It was inevitable that eventually the Tong would also arrive."

"For what purpose?" Ki wondered.

"Presumably to extort money from my brother, the way they demand payment from all Chinese businesses. They wanted to prove that a Chinese could never run far enough to escape the rule of the Tong. But they also wanted Zen Mo to acknowledge their supremacy, and bow to their will. A strong man like my brother, even living out here, is, as far as the Tong is concerned, a bad influence on others."

"They didn't want him to become a good role model to others, so they made an example out of him," Ki said.

"Exactly. Zen Mo understood that. And he would have fought. But he would have lost more than he would have gained."

"I don't see how. . . ."

"You don't realize how important the Double C is to us. Men could come here and be proud. They weren't coolies or houseboys anymore, they were real honest-to-goodness cowboys. That may seem silly, but . . ."

"There's nothing silly about that," Ki assured her.

"And my brother didn't want to lose that opportunity. Not for himself; he was already as tough a cowhand as you'd ever meet," she said with a bittersweet smile, "but for the others that were yet to follow. Zen Mo had no choice but to give in."

Ki started to say something, but she cut him off. "There was no other way, Ki," she continued with a shake of her head. "Once Scott knew about the Tong, he would never trust another Chinese. He would wonder about every new hand that came looking for a job. Each new man could be an agent of the Tong, sent here to corrupt his crew."

"I see your point," Ki conceded.

"It started out as only a token gesture. The Tong took only so much, so as to prove their dominance. Zen Mo balanced it out by making sure the crew was hard-working." She chuckled to herself. "They were not only hard-working; they were the best. Zen Mo often said they worked so hard they more than made up for what the Tong took."

"Then what happened?"

"My brother died." She saw Ki's expression and added quickly, "Of consumption."

"To bring a long story to a close, Tsen-ti took over, and the Tong began to exert more influence. When it became known that Mr. Scott was going to sell the ranch, the Tong decided they wanted the Double C for their own. They found little opposition in the bunkhouse."

"For fear their families would be punished," Ki remarked.

"Not only that, but they also feared for their jobs. With the exception of Jessie, not many would keep on a Chinese crew. It was easy to look the other way."

"It's hard to see the Tong as the lesser of two evils."

"No one wanted to go back to the crowded streets of Chinatown," Ling Ling explained. "But then you showed up, and Jessie assured the men they would still have jobs. . . ."

"And that's when Chan tried to kill Scott. He had to get the ranch before it became Jessie's." Ling Ling nodded. Ki thought a moment. "Unwittingly, Jessie almost signed Scott's death warrant."

"I don't understand," Ling Ling confessed.

"When Jessie told the men that the ranch would be hers as soon as Scott returned with the papers, Chan knew he had to act. One more question. Why did Tsen-ti die?" Ki hated to ask it, but he had to know.

"I think he drew the line at murder. Scott was a good friend to the Chinese, and an even better friend to Tsen-ti. Tsen-ti couldn't stand by and let harm come to Scott."

"And what now, Ling Ling?"

"I don't know. I can only speak for myself. I will avenge the murder of my cousin."

The words cut Ki like a knife. "No, Ling Ling. You can't."

Ling Ling knew his thoughts. "I am not Su Ling, Ki. I won't sacrifice my life to the Tong."

Ki hardly heard. He stood up slowly. His head felt light, his heart heavy. Would fate play this trick on him again? Was history destined to repeat itself? As hard as he tried, he couldn't get the vision of Su Ling out of his mind. Su Ling, as she hurled herself with deadly purpose. Su Ling, as the Tong bodyguards riddled her body with their deadly bullets.

Ling Ling could see the pain on Ki's face. She wanted to reassure him that she would do nothing foolish. "There is no victory in death," she said slowly. "Especially for one in love."

Ki didn't respond. He looked down at her, and beyond her. Finally he spoke, his voice sounding very far away. "No harm will come to you. I will destroy Chan Pei."

It was not a promise or a threat. It was a man caught in a destiny that held no escape.

It was almost noon before Jessie got out of bed. They had been up for hours, but were otherwise engaged until now.

After a quick meal of ham and biscuits, it was time to part. "I really do have to be getting back," Jessie said with regret.

"I understand," Mercer said. "I should be on the range with my men, too. But when will I see you again?"

"We're neighbors, remember? I'll be dropping by to pay a neighborly call."

"But I mean really see you, Jessie." He said it with just the right emphasis, so there was no mistaking his meaning.

"See ya 'round the dance halls, partner," she said with a twinkle. "That is of course if you decide to choose me. . . ."

He scooped her into his arms and kissed her hard. "I can't imagine there being another."

"Now I know that can't be true, Mercer. But I appreciate the thought, nonetheless."

"There'll never be one like you," he said sincerely. Jessie accepted that as the truth.

With his arm around her waist he walked her out to the barn.

They had just crossed into the dark interior when the wood post smacked violently between Mercer's shoulderblades. It was wielded with such force that the rancher was unconscious even before his head smashed into the packed dirt floor of the barn.

• • •

Ki did not delay. He left without a word to Scott. Ling Ling was right. There was no reason to bring any of this to his attention. The Double C was a Starbuck ranch now. They took care of their own. Besides, the man needed his rest. Though his wound was healing, after his foreman's death Scott had become weak and developed a high fever.

Ki started a hundred yards from the corral and began cutting for sign, by moving in ever widening concentric circles. There were many tracks, and it was difficult to determine those that were left by Chan Pei and his men. Finally he came upon a set of prints that appeared to be reasonably fresh. He followed those. Soon he could make out seven distinct sets of hoofprints.

He wasn't certain he was on the right track, but he would stay on it either till he found Chan or till the trail dried up. He packed enough rice to last for days; he also packed Scott's repeating carbine, in addition to the Colt that was still in his saddlebag. That he was even carrying those firearms was a good indication of his state of mind.

But the slow process of tracking helped to calm him. He considered the options. More than likely Chan Pei wished to elevate his status in the Tong. To avenge the death of Tong leader Steel Claw would certainly do that. To defeat the man who dealt a blow to the Tong would be a feather in Chan's cap. If Chan could also secure the Double C for the Tong he would become a highly respected, powerful leader in his own right.

Ki was sure that Chan knew who he was. The telegram from San Francisco would supply him with the information on Jessie and himself. . . .

Ki stopped short. Jessie and the Starbuck empire had also been responsible for the Tong's defeat. Ki had to remember that it wasn't his own personal battle. Chan would no doubt wreak his revenge on her as well. He had been so preoccupied with his own bitter thoughts and with Ling Ling's welfare that he had almost overlooked Jessie.

He had to think this through, and quickly. He had to put himself in Chan Pei's shoes. The man wanted to win at any cost. He would stop at nothing to attain his goal. But he was a coward. It was unlikely he would face Ki directly, man to man. Ki began to tense even before the truth seized him.

The best way to ensure victory was to strike at the least guarded point. The weakest link of the chain was the first to break. And even the strongest chain was rendered useless if but one link broke.

The strength of Ki, the power and wealth of the Starbuck empire mattered little if Chan got to Jessie.

Ki turned his horse in the direction of the Lazy M, and dug his spurs into the animal's sides.

Jessie reacted quickly, going right for her sixgun. But just as she was sliding it out of its holster, two powerful arms grabbed her and held her fast.

"There will be no need for that, Miss Starbuck," a voice from the shadows said calmly. Chan Pei stepped forward and, grinning, took her gun and placed it into his waistband.

"You could have killed him," she said furiously. "Now let me go."

"He is of no concern to us," Chan Pei said in answer to her first remark. Her second he ignored totally.

Jessie fumed. "As long as I own the Double C there'll be no more fight with Mercer."

Chan laughed nastily. "We are about to change all that, Miss Starbuck."

He was interrupted by two other Chinese entering the barn. "The bunkhouse is empty," one informed him.

"I don't know what you're up to, but I demand you let go of me. At once."

Chan nodded, and the arms that pinned her fell away.

"We will go up to the house and I will explain," Chan

161

said with a cold, evil grin. He gave Mercer the briefest look. "Tie him," he commanded.

They sat Jessie down at the table, the four Chinese plug-uglies surrounding her. Chan stood before her. "I will get right to the point. I desire the Double C. You will sell it to me." He pulled out a neatly folded piece of paper and handed it to her.

Jessie read the paper. It was a legally binding sale contract. "That's a fair price," she said, referring to the figure on the agreement.

Chan reached into his vest pocket and pulled out an envelope. "A bank draft, made out for the full amount."

"But what if I choose not to sell?" Jessie had a feeling that once she signed the agreement, she would never live to see the money, if in fact the envelope really did hold a draft.

Chan snapped his fingers. One of the plug-uglies placed a bottle of ink on the table. Another thrust a quill into her hands.

"You will sign." Chan Pei seemed confident.

Jessie did not dare ask how he could be so certain. She had no doubt there were evil and quite effective means at his disposal. It was best to play innocent and try to stall for time. "Even if I do, the deal won't be binding. Ki would also have to sign. He's half-owner."

Chan's face darkened. His eyes narrowed. "A dead owner is no owner at all."

Jessie assumed he was referring to Ki, not herself, though it made no difference. "I won't scare easily. If you kill me you'll lose any chance of getting the ranch. My lawyers already have a copy of the bill of sale." Though it wasn't true, there was no way Chan could know that. Jessie was starting to think that she had him blocked at every turn.

Chan seemed unfazed. He reached into his pocket and pulled out his ornate silver dagger. Unconsciously, Jessie tensed. Chan noticed and smiled. "You may prove to be quite brave, Miss Starbuck," he said as he casually cleaned his nails with the sharp point.

The bull-headed Chinaman pulled out his knife as well. He smiled cruelly, revealing two missing teeth. "Let me start on her," he said eagerly.

"No." Chan's voice was sharp. "There may be no need for that." He smiled at Jessie. "I would hate to mar such beauty. I would much rather you go to your grave looking every bit as beautiful as you did in life."

"You won't kill me," Jessie said with a confidence she didn't possess. "I'm no good to you dead."

"You are no good to me alive either, unless you sign that paper."

Jessie remained silent but looked defiantly at him.

"As I see, you no doubt are brave, Miss Starbuck, but we will see how strong you are in the face of another's pain and suffering." He turned to his men. "Tie her up, then get me the *Jibon-ren,*" he instructed.

Jessie cursed herself silently. Why did she have to involve Ki? She thought she was so smart, naming him as a co-owner, but now the plan had backfired. It would have been better to sign the paper right off, and take her chances. Perhaps she still could. "There's no need to get Ki . . ." she began.

Chan Pei smiled at her. "I do not care whether he is a part owner or not." Apparently he saw through her scheme. "I have a score to settle. And it will please me to have you present," he said sadistically.

A man returned with rope. He grabbed Jessie's arms and tied them tightly behind her back. "He'll kill you," she stated plainly, as another bound her feet.

Chan Pei remained calm. "He will no doubt try." He turned to the bull-headed one. "Remember, I want the barbarian alive!"

The man looked uneasy. "It may not be so easy. . . ."

163

Another plug-ugly nodded his agreement.

"Weaklings." Chan spat out the word, then smiled slowly. "But you may be right. "We will send for him. When the rancher comes to his senses . . ."

"Will he come, just because Mercer asks it?" questioned one of the Chinese.

"When he hears we have the woman, the barbarian will come running." He smiled ominously as he stroked the sharp edge of the dagger. "And we will be waiting."

★

Chapter 15

Ki rode into the Lazy M corral and brought his horse to a quick stop.

"Jessie! Mercer!" he called loudly from the saddle. There seemed to be no sign of them. He was about to dismount and check the house when he decided not to waste any time. He headed straight for the barn to see if their mounts were in the stalls.

He ducked his head and rode into the barn. He saw Jessie's horse and assumed she must be walking the hills with Mercer. He turned to exit, when he caught sight of the lump. He couldn't believe he almost missed it.

Ki slid down from the saddle and rushed over to where Mercer's body was slumped against the wall. The rancher was barely conscious. "Mercer, what happened?" Ki asked as he shook the man by the shoulders. Immediately, he felt something askew with the rancher's right shoulder. A quick look showed the bone to be badly dislocated, or broken, or both. With a *shuriken* blade Ki cut through the ropes and gently placed Mercer on his side.

"Mercer, can you hear me?" Ki asked as he slapped the man's face.

"There ain't nothing wrong with my hearin'. You don't have to hit me ag'in."

"What happened? Where's Jessie?"

"She was with me. Why, what happened? Where is she?" It was his turn to ask. He started to sit up and groaned in pain.

"You don't remember?"

Mercer shook his head. "I stepped into the barn, and that was the last thing I can recall."

Ki rose to his feet. "Stay here. Your shoulder's broken. I'm going up to the house," he said, then ran out.

His speed saved him.

They were waiting for him outside the barn. But they didn't expect him to come bursting out. The plug-ugly with the fence post took a good swing, but he was too slow. The beam caught Ki with just a glancing blow. Ki stumbled forward, and, unable to check himself, tucked in his head and went into a quick roll.

Two Chinamen lunged at him—or rather, where they thought he was. Ki was up on his feet while they were grabbing at dirt. Ki pivoted quickly and brought back his right foot. He swung it hard into the first plug-ugly's face. The second Chinaman was just getting up when Ki drove both fists deep into the man's gut.

Ki turned in time to see the fence post come swinging towards his head. He raised his hands instinctively, caught the pole, and dropped to his back. His assailant went flying past, but managed to hang on to his weapon. A man strong enough to wield the heavy post would not have it torn from his grasp that easily. He regained his feet and turned back to Ki.

166

There was a good eight feet separating them. Enough space, and enough time, to get off one throw. Ki rarely needed more than one chance. His fingers dug into his vest pocket and came up flashing silver. The *shuriken* sped on its way. . . .

. . . And buried itself halfway into the wood post. By sheer luck the Chinaman happened to be lifting the beam at the exact moment the throwing star was zooming towards the target. Instead of cutting flesh, it harmlessly splintered wood.

The fence post again came bearing down on Ki. Ki backed up cautiously. A hit anywhere could easily break a bone.

Arms locked around him. The second plug-ugly had regained his breath, and grabbed Ki from behind. Fence Post moved closer. Ki dug his thumb into the hand that was locked around his chest. His fingers closed like a vise, and twisted the wrist back. The hold broken, the hand peeled away effortlessly. Still holding the wrist, Ki swung the Chinaman around.

The post moved in a fast arc and collided, with thunderous impact, into the skull of the Chinaman. Blood and brains splattered Ki. It was chance that had the plug-ugly stop the blow meant for Ki. Luck had balanced out.

Before Fence Post could bring his weapon around for another blow, Ki dove headfirst into the man's stomach. They toppled to the ground. At close quarters the post was useless. It took a second for Fence Post to realize that. It was a second too long.

Ki kept his weight pressed against the man, and quickly managed to get one hand free. This time the *shuriken* would find the mark. Ki was certain. The throwing star never left his hand. In one clean swipe he sliced it across Fence Post's jugular. The man's luck had run out.

Ki turned in time to see the very first plug-ugly, his face a bloody mess, come at him with a dagger.

Ki reacted swiftly. The bloody *shuriken* went sailing

through the air. It buried itself deep into the man's chest. With a gasp the plug-ugly fell face down to the dirt.

Nervously, Ki took a quick mental count. There were two dead, one possibly still alive. . . .

"Very good, barbarian."

Ki turned to face the bull-headed Chinaman. Relieved, Ki smiled to himself. He needed one alive. Bull-head would be the one.

The Chinaman, brandishing a pitchfork, closed the distance quickly. "Chan wants you alive." He jabbed the pitchfork menacingly. "A man can live with many holes, but he won't live long."

Instinctively, Ki sensed Bull-head to be the best fighter. The fact that he had the wisdom to stand back and let the other plug-uglies get in each other's way attested to that. Coupled with the fact that he wanted the Chinaman alive, Ki would have to move with extreme caution, both offensively and defensively.

They circled each other carefully, Bull-head waiting patiently to strike.

"Hey, Chinaman!" The call came from behind. "Yeah, you, fathead!"

Bull-head turned quickly to steal a look.

A gun exploded.

The Chinaman fell backwards, a hole in the center of his chest. "Damn!" Ki cursed loudly.

"Sorry, Ki. I never could shoot a man in the back." The rancher lay in the doorway of the barn, a smoking sixgun in his hand. Though he was smiling it was evident that he was in much pain. "In my condition they never bothered taking my six-shooter."

Ki raced to the man with the *shuriken* in his chest. The one that might still be breathing. He turned him over gently, but the man was dead.

Ki stepped past Mercer, went into the barn, and pulled his carbine from the saddle boot.

"Is that all the thanks I get?" the rancher began.

"I was hoping one of them would live long enough to tell me where Jessie is," Ki said with just a trace of anger, as he passed the rancher again on the way out.

Mercer said nothing.

Inside the ranch house Chan heard the shot. He cursed in Chinese, then turned to one of his men. "See how it goes. The barbarian had better be alive or they will pay dearly," he swore viciously.

Rifle in hand, Ki climbed the windmill. Were the plug-uglies left behind to trap him, or were Chan and Jessie still somewhere on the ranch? From the top of the tower he could quickly survey the grounds and perhaps find an answer. Either way his position on the tower had tactical advantages.

Ki was hoping to spot their horses, and by a simple count determine the whereabouts of Chan. He had tracked seven horses; four men were dead. . . . But he couldn't locate a single mount. They must be tethered at the far side of the barn, out of sight.

He turned to the ranch house to see if he could detect any movement inside the building.

He heard the creak first, then caught sight of the door swinging open. He brought his rifle up to his shoulder, steadied it, and took aim.

The Chinaman took one step out of the house. The rifle cracked sharply. The man dropped—a small ugly hole piercing the top of his head.

Chan heard the shot and the thump as the body hit the porch.

He went to Jessie, cut her legs free, and hoisted her to her feet. He wrapped one arm around her upper chest and thrust her in front of him. His other hand held the dagger to her throat, its point making a slight indentation in her soft skin.

Chan addressed the other Chinaman, the last of his

plug-uglies. "Wait for the barbarian," he ordered. "Wound him if you can. Kill him if you must."

Jessie's body tensed. Her mind raced, looking for a way to warn Ki.

Walking behind her, Chan pushed them to the door. "One sound, the slightest struggle, and your life ends," he whispered in her ear.

Ki saw them step out. He wavered momentarily, but kept the rifle on target.

After a moment, Chan spotted his adversary atop the tower. "Drop the gun, barbarian!"

"You are a dead man," Ki called back calmly.

"Drop the gun or she dies," Chan repeated.

"If I do, she dies anyway."

"There are quick, merciful ways to die, and slow, painful ways," Chan said ominously. His meaning was clear.

"Exactly," Ki agreed. "We barbarians know of torture you civilized people never dreamed of," he said with a slight touch of sarcasm. "Harm her, and you will learn this firsthand. I promise you an excruciating death, Chan."

The tall Chinaman smiled. "A treed fox should not hurl threats at the hunter."

"Let her go, Chan, and you can walk away with your life."

Chan shrugged. "You lose if she dies," he said simply.

"I can put a bullet between your eyes before your dagger cuts her throat." It was not a simple boast.

"It is a sporting proposition, barbarian. A challenge I'd take you up on. But I don't think you will risk it." He was calling Ki's bluff. "Perhaps some other time." Chan started to lead Jessie around the back of the house.

But was it a bluff? Ki sighted down the barrel. His height advantage from the windmill gave Ki a clear shot at the top of Chan's head. He wouldn't miss. Of that he was certain. If Chan slumped forward, Jessie would remain un-

injured. But if the Chinaman toppled over backwards . . .
Ki couldn't risk it.

Chan, though, was still wary of a sudden change of
mind on Ki's part. He called out to his lackey. "Lee, get
out here. Bring our horses."

The man emerged from the building. Ki trained the rifle
on him and felt the urge to pull the trigger. But he didn't. If
he made Chan's escape difficult, or if he pushed the Chinaman too hard, Chan might decide to kill Jessie on the spot.

Helplessly, Ki watched as Lee fetched the horses. Taking their time, the group walked slowly out of rifle range,
where they mounted up. Chan and Jessie shared one horse.

Ki stood on the windmill and watched them disappear
into the hills before climbing down and mounting his own
horse.

There was no rush. Ki could not overtake them. If he
tried, Jessie's life would again be in danger. He had to take
them by surprise, coming upon them by stealth. The trail
was easy to follow, as Chan was making no effort to lose
Ki. Ki turned this over in his mind. The Chinaman was no
doubt preparing a surprise of his own.

Chan stopped finally at a line camp. He and his lackey
brought Jessie in, tied her to the cot, then left. Jessie could
hear Chan issue instructions though she couldn't make out
the words. A moment later Chan re-entered the shack.

He turned a chair to face Jessie, then sat down. He
removed a small silver case, from which he took a cigarette
holder and a hand-rolled smoke. He moved very deliber-
ately, almost ceremonially. He struck a match and puffed
slowly on the tobacco-herb mixture. Acrid smoke filled the
room. Chan watched it spiral to the ceiling, then turned his
attention to Jessie.

"I'd like to thank you, Miss Starbuck. You have given
me an opportunity I am truly grateful for." His tone was
quite sincere.

171

"Then let me go."

Chan smiled. "Regrettably, I cannot do that."

"As long as you keep me, Ki will continue to hunt you."

"Precisely."

"You can't win, Chan."

"But I already have." Chan smiled. There was no malice in his smile. It was genuine, and that frightened Jessie all the more. "There is nothing more to do but wait." With that he closed his eyes.

Jessie watched Chan. She had seen the same blank expression on Ki's face during his meditations. She struggled with her ropes, but it was no use; they were tied securely. She lay back and rested. She might need her strength later.

The day wore on, and Ki became worried. Had he guessed wrong? He assumed the Chinaman would lay a trap for him, but was Chan actually trying to escape with Jessie? Chan had vowed vengeance on Ki. What better way to make Ki suffer than to let him live, knowing that Jessie was captive in a smoke-filled opium den somewhere in Chinatown, a slave to the warlords of the Tong?

Fear gripped Ki's soul, and he had to fight hard to control it. Chan Pei knew Ki would never rest till he saved Jessie. He would not be so stupid as to bring Ki's vengeance down on the Lords of the Tong. Or would he? Then and there Ki vowed he would live to make Chan Pei suffer —horribly.

A squirrel's frantic chirping pulled Ki from his macabre thoughts. The rodent was too far off to be upset by Ki's coming. It was something else. Ki stopped and listened carefully. The field was quiet save for the squirrel. The small animal was warning his brothers: danger, an intruder. Ki took heed.

Silently, he slipped down from the saddle. Moving cautiously, he stepped off the trail and made his way towards the tree where the squirrel was. He was more than halfway to that point when he stopped and picked up a small stone.

He threw it at his horse, hitting the animal in the rump. The horse moved forward.

Ki got his *shurikens* ready: two in his right hand, two in his left. His horse walked past. Ki waited, listening. Then he heard it, from a bush to his right. The click of a revolver hammer being drawn back. He let the *shurikens* fly into the shrub. One was a little high to the right corner, the other to the left corner. He hurled a throwing star into each quadrant. There was a crash in the bush, and the last of the plug-uglies pitched over, dead.

That left only Chan Pei.

Chan Pei opened his eyes. "Lee has not returned," he remarked to no one in particular. "That means your friend the barbarian will be here shortly." He rose from the table, then leaned over and lit the oil lamp. He picked it up and drew back his arm.

Jessie stared in fright. His intentions were obvious. "Wait! If you kill me you'll never get the ranch."

"There are other ranches," he said stoically.

"But why?" Jessie was truly puzzled. Other than wanting the Double C for his own, what grudge did Chan Pei have with her? Why would he kill her so ruthlessly?

"For the honor of my family."

"I don't understand . . ." Jessie began.

"To avenge my uncle's death."

Jessie was still puzzled.

"You ruined him; the barbarian killed him. He ripped out his heart."

Jessie gasped. If Chan Pei meant what he said . . . She had seen Ki kill a man like that, a Tong leader in San Francisco. . . .

"So you remember Steel Claw. He was my uncle. Now you understand."

Jessie knew there was nothing she could say.

"I could have lived my whole life never avenging the death of my uncle. There is nothing I value more."

He threw the lamp into the corner. It shattered loudly, spilling oil on the wall and floor. An instant later tendrils of flame shot out along the oiled pathways.

"Goodbye, Miss Starbuck." With that Chan Pei left, closing the door behind him.

Ki saw the first wisps of smoke and thought it was from Chan's campsite. He raced in that direction, and as he broke out into the meadow, he practically ran over Chan Pei.

The Chinaman seemed to be waiting for him. He stood in a classic fighting position and barred Ki's way. "Now it is just us, barbarian."

"Is she alive?" Ki demanded.

"She is alive, but not for long."

Ki regretted leaving the guns in his saddlebag. He would not have hesitated to shoot the man where he stood. He also regretted that he had no more *shurikens*. He used his last ones on the lackey, and uncharacteristically was in such haste he did not bother to retrieve them.

But it did not matter. Ki would take him with his bare hands. It might take longer, but it would not be without its satisfaction.

Ki struck quickly with a snap kick to the head. But Chan, unlike most American adversaries, was not taken by surprise. He was not fooled by such an 'unorthodox' move. He stepped to the side, and blocked the kick with his forearm.

"This is our final contest, barbarian," Chan Pei said proudly.

"It will be your downfall."

"There are new rules," Chan said with a smile.

"The outcome will be the same," Ki promised, as he let loose with a spinning kick. Chan blocked this as well.

"Perhaps," the Chinaman said slowly. "But I get to toy with you. I get to watch your suffering."

Up till now, Ki was feeling out his opponent, seeing how he reacted. Now it was time to strike. Ki moved in, leading again with a snap kick to the head, and as expected, Chan Pei stepped to the side, and prepared to block with his forearm. But before contact was made, Ki brought back his leg, dropped it under Chan's arm, and struck solidly to the chest. The Chinaman staggered back.

"Very good, barbarian. Let the contest begin," he announced. "You try and get to the shack before it burns, and I"—he kicked at Ki—"I try and stop you."

"Jessie!" Ki cried out. He came at Chan Pei in a flurry of exploding kicks and jabs. Some hit their mark, but the Chinaman held his ground.

Now it was Chan Pei's turn. He was as skilled at offense as he was at defense. Perhaps even better. He was every bit as tall as Ki, with a good, long leg extension. His rapid-fire kicks kept Ki at bay.

"You see, barbarian, I have already won."

It was true. If Ki couldn't get around him soon it would be too late to save Jessie. Ki couldn't afford to trade blows with him. He had to end this quickly.

The foot seemed to come out of nowhere. Ki was taken by surprise by the high flying kick. He saw it, but too late. It exploded in his face with thundering impact.

He got quickly to his feet, but was clearly demoralized.

Chan Pei laughed heartily. "Do not fret, barbarian. With any luck the smoke will choke her lungs before the flames burn her flesh."

The taunt served to weaken Ki further. Chan struck again. Ki blocked the right front kick, but the left foot snapped hard against his hip. He lost his balance momentarily and Chan, unrelenting, connected with a spinning kick to the side of the head.

The sharp pain helped clear Ki's thoughts. Chan Pei was skilled with his feet. Painfully so. But he was not as good with his hands. Their last meeting had proved that. Ki could no longer keep his distance. To gain the advantage he had to close in. But it would not be simple. Chan Pei was clearly his equal.

A side kick shot out quickly. This time Ki did not try to avoid it. He prepared himself for the impact and let it connect. But as Chan drew his leg back, Ki grabbed hold of it. Using it for leverage he leaned back and drove his foot deep into Chan's kidney. As long as he had hold of Chan's leg the Chinaman's side was open and defenseless. Ki brought his leg back and again snapped it quickly into Chan's kidney. He almost managed one more kick before Chan twisted around and caught Ki behind the head with his other foot. They toppled over.

Ki scrambled to his feet and started to make a run to the shack. He had gone two steps before a low ankle sweep brought him back to the ground. Before he fell he caught sight of the flames that now enveloped the wood structure.

As Ki lay there a foot smashed into his ribs. He didn't care. The fight had gone out of him. He had failed Jessie. He had failed in his duty. He had lost. He had lost a major part of himself.

There was another kick to the ribs, but he barely felt the pain, so consumed was he with emotional anguish. A foot rolled him on to his back. Chan Pei's hideous face peered down at him and scoffed. "You are beaten, barbarian."

Ki knew it was so. He thought briefly of Ling Ling. What was it she had said? There is no victory in death. Especially for one in love. *Forgive me, Ling Ling. I did love, but perhaps not enough. In death there is honor. Maybe. But surely their is a respite from the guilt, the torment, and the pain. . . .*

"You will die." Chan Pei dove at him, dagger in hand.

And Ki reacted automatically. He grabbed the wrist firmly and brought his leg up into the Chinaman's back. Chan rolled over him, and Ki scurried to his feet.

Impatient for the kill, Chan Pei lunged at Ki. Moving with a newfound speed, Ki again caught hold of Chan's

176

wrist. But this time he didn't let go. His other hand delivered a powerful *teisho,* the heel of the hand striking Chan's forearm full strength.

He heard the bone crack. The dagger dropped away. But Ki still held on to the wrist.

He made a lightning quick *yoko-geri-kea* to the kidney, his foot snapping forcefully into the already weakened organ. He brought his foot back and again struck with devastating results. Chan Pei staggered, standing only because Ki held his wrist.

Then Ki let go, and the Chinaman slumped to his knees. Ki brought his right arm back for a *yonhon-nukite.* He put more force behind this spear-hand strike than any blow he could recall. His fingers punctured the skin above the diaphragm. Ki felt the warm, sticky blood coat his hand. Chan's eyes bulged. He gasped in excruciating pain. Ki's fingers gripped tighter. He was about to pull out the Chinaman's entrails, but he stopped. He slid his hand out from the man's gut.

I am not a barbarian, he told himself. He stepped back. "You are beaten, Chan Pei," he said calmly, then leaped into the air. In one powerful kick, a beautifully executed *mae-tobi-geri* Ki snapped Chan Pei's neck.

★

Chapter 16

Ki felt anything but victorious.

Then he looked up and thought he was hallucinating. Jessie was running towards him. Behind her were Ling Ling and the crew of the Double C.

Then he felt Ling Ling in his arms and he knew it wasn't a dream.

His thoughts fogged up; his eyes became cloudy. He barely understood what was being said.

Apparently, Ling Ling had convinced the others that with Ki as their champion this was the time to stand up to the Tong. Hong organized the men, and they took off in search of Chan Pei. They were riding the range when they saw the smoke of the burning line camp.

Tommy was the first one on the scene. He had a debt to

pay. He dashed in and pulled Jessie from the flames. "After all," he said with a smile, "I learned it from Ki."

On the way back to the ranch, Ki explained everything to Jessie.

"One question, Ki. That first day, when the crew was being shot at by rustlers—"

"It was all staged to discourage any prospective buyers."

"But the poisoned water holes?"

"To encourage Scott to unload the ranch quickly."

"It came very close to working," she remarked dryly. "And what about Mercer?" She asked after a moment's thought.

"His shoulder looks to be broken, but other than that . . ."

"I think I may pay a neighborly call on Mr. Mercer before we head back to the Circle Star." She looked apologetic. "We do have to be getting back, Ki."

He understood.

All night they lay in bed. Talking, loving, thinking. By morning they understood each other, though Ki couldn't distinguish what he had said from what Ling Ling had said. But that was unimportant. For the first time, matters of his heart were clearly in focus.

Time had magnified the memory of Su Ling, and the more he tried to block out that memory the larger it became.

"Time will again reduce it. Su Ling was just a woman," someone had said.

"A woman of the past," the other voice said.

"It is a deep wound, recently reopened. . . ."

"But a wound ready to heal."

"It will take time. . . ."

That night they had all the time in the world. And they made love again.

With the sun streaming in, Ling Ling kissed Ki's forehead. "When you rid yourself of the others and free yourself from your duty, then perhaps I will be here still. Waiting."

The wagon bounced down the road. Ki turned for one final look. He could see Ling Ling standing on the porch. *The time will come. Then I will return.* . . .

Watch for

LONE STAR AND THE OUTLAW POSSE

sixtieth novel of the exciting
LONE STAR
series from Jove

coming in August!